THE
GUNSMITH
GIANT

THE
INDEPENDENCE DAY GANG

A Giant Holiday Gunsmith Adventure

THE GUNSMITH GIANT

THE INDEPENDENCE DAY GANG

A Giant Holiday Gunsmith Adventure

J.R. Roberts

SPEAKING VOLUMES, LLC
NAPLES, FLORIDA
2022

The Independence Day Gang

ISBN 978-1-64540-770-6

Chapter One

June 30

The sound of children crying permeated the night air. This did not please Trevor Henry.

"Shut those kids up," he told his number one man, Lyle Kent.

"You say that every year, boss," Kent said. "They're kids, and they're scared. Maybe we should start taking older kids."

"Three to five are in demand, you know that," Henry said. "We'll stick with them. Tell Lily I want her."

"Right."

Kent, a man in his thirties, walked away and returned with Lily Palmer in tow. Lily was in her early thirties and in charge of the children.

"I know, I know," she said, "you want them to be quiet."

"If you know that, then do it," Henry snapped.

"Are we stopping in Temple City?"

"We stop there every year," he told her.

"I know, on the Fourth of July," she said. "You don't think they know that, by now?"

"Temple City is my lucky stop," he told her. "You know that. We make a good haul there and have luck the rest of the way to Galveston."

"Yeah, right."

"I'm gettin' some coffee."

As Trevor Henry walked away, Kent came over and stood by Lily.

"His superstition is gonna be the death of us," Lily said.

"Not as long as it keeps workin'," Kent said.

"I think we're pushin' it, goin' back along this route five years in a row."

"Trevor's the boss," Kent said.

"Right."

Henry came walking back, carrying a cup of coffee.

"Are we ready for tomorrow?" he asked.

"The schoolhouse outside of Maryville," Lily said.

"Right."

"Yeah, we're set," Kent said. "I'll be taking Hawk and Taylor."

"Good," Henry said.

"Since it's a schoolhouse," Kent said, "we'll only be gettin' fives and sixes."

"That's okay," Henry said. "As usual, we'll clean up in Temple City on the Fourth."

Kent and Lily didn't comment.

"Lyle, set the watches," Kent ordered. "Then tell everyone to turn in."

"Right."

Henry looked at Lily.

"Watch after those kids and keep 'em quiet."

"I'll try."

Henry carried his coffee to his own bed roll, finished it and tried to get some sleep.

***

In Temple City, Texas, the townspeople were getting ready for their Fourth of July celebration.

Sheriff Sam Cade stood in front of his office, sipping coffee and watching his neighbors decorate. They had already strung a large sign across the main street that said FOURTH OF JULY CELEBRATION!

" 'mornin', Sheriff."

Dalton turned and saw Simon Crawford, a member of the town council, approaching. Crawford owned the feed store in town.

"Simon," Dalton greeted.

Crawford stood alongside the lawman.

"So, whataya think?"

"About what?"

"The decorations."

"That's pretty much what the town does every year," the sheriff said.

"And what about the Independence Day Gang?"

Dalton scowled.

"Come on, Sheriff," Crawford said. "It's four years in a row now that some of our kids have come up missing on the Fourth of July."

"And how stupid would it be for such a gang to try it five years in a row?"

"Aren't criminals usually stupid?" Crawford asked. "And arrogant?"

"It certainly would be arrogant for them to try it a fifth year in a row."

"Well," Crawford said, "at least this time you'll be ready for them." He slapped the lawman on the back. "We have confidence in you, Sheriff."

Crawford walked on. Sheriff Dalton dumped the remainder of his coffee on the street and went into his office.

Chapter Two

July 1

Clint woke the morning of July first. He was usually on the trail for Independence Day, but he was thinking of making sure he was in a town for some festivities this year.

He was in the town of South Council, which was located between Maryville and Temple City. Folks in South Council told him that Temple City was the place to be on the 4th, so that was where he was planning to go.

But this morning he was in bed with a woman named Maggie Prescott. They had met the night before in a local café, were immediately attracted to each other. Clint moved to her table, and by the time their meal had been consumed, they agreed to go to his room together.

Maggie turned onto her back and stretched her sleek body. It was unusual to Clint that he found himself interested in her, as she was tall and slender, with almost no breasts. Once she was naked, though, he saw how lovely her sleekness was, small teacup breasts with large, brown nipples. Her hair was long and auburn, and the bush between her legs slightly lighter.

When she saw him watching her, she smiled.

"Good morning," she said.

"Good morning. How did you sleep?"

"Like a log," she said. "You?"

"The same."

"You know why, don't you?" she asked. "We wore each other out."

"Yes, we did."

She reached over and slid her hand onto his chest and belly.

"Too worn out for a morning repast?"

He turned toward her and slid his hand down onto her hip.

"Not at all . . ."

Their limbs entwined, their skin rubbing together inflamed both of them once again. Clint drove his rock hard cock into her wet pussy, which sucked him in willingly. She wrapped those long legs around him, found his rhythm and matched it, swaying her hips in unison with his thrusts, and it went on like that for a long time . . .

***

Maggie rolled off Clint onto her back, breathing deeply.

"Oh, my," she said.

"Oh, yes," he said.

"We did it again," she said. "I'm worn out."

"So am I," he said. "This was a considerable night and morning to remember."

"Are you leaving town?" she asked.

"Yes," he said, "this morning."

"Do you have time for breakfast?"

"Yes, I do," he said. "Time for a long breakfast."

She got up to get dressed and caught him watching her.

"Are you going to get dressed," she asked, "or just watch me?"

"I thought I'd do both."

She frowned at him, and then turned her back to dress. He shrugged, stood and got dressed himself. When she turned back to him, he was strapping on his gun.

"Shall we go?" he asked.

"I'm feeling kind of grimy," she said, "but after breakfast I'll go back to my own room and wash up."

"And I'll mount my horse and ride out."

"Where to?" she asked.

"A town called Temple City," he said.

"Is it important to you?" she asked.

"Not at all," he said. "It simply comes next." He opened the door. "Shall we go?"

7

***

They ate breakfast in the hotel dining room, off the lobby.

"How long will you be in Temple City?" she asked.

"Possibly til the next day. And which way are you going?"

"The opposite direction," she said. "I'm not sure where I'm headed, exactly, but I like to travel."

"As do I," he said.

"And where will you be on the Fourth, when the fireworks go off?" she asked.

"I have no idea," he said. "That kind of display has never been important to me."

"To me neither, but I'll be looking up at the skies and thinking of you. After all, we've made our own fireworks, haven't we?"

"We sure have," he said, smiling.

***

After breakfast she kissed him in the lobby, while others watched. Then she went to her own room to freshen up, while he went to go to the livery to claim his horse and ride out of town.

Chapter Three

When Trevor Henry woke on July first, he felt the usual thrill of that day. First day of July was special to him, almost as special as July Fourth.

He stood up and walked to the fire where Del Brandon, who cooked for the gang, was pouring coffee.

"Here ya go, boss," he said, handing Henry a cup.

"Thanks, Del."

"Breakfast in ten minutes," Del said.

"Sounds good."

Brandon had been riding with Henry longer than anyone and was always treated well by the gang leader. That was because Trevor Henry never wanted to mistreat the man who was in charge of his food.

Henry turned to see Kent approaching. That was when he noticed the silence.

"Where are the kids?" he asked.

"Lily's got 'em," Kent said. "She managed to shut them up."

Kent accepted a cup of coffee from Brandon. Then he and Henry moved away from the fire to make room for others.

"Are they all ours?" Henry asked, indicating the men lined up for coffee and breakfast.

"You hired them all, boss," Kent said. "Don't you remember?"

Henry looked at him blankly for a moment, then his face changed.

"Of course I remember!" he snapped. But then he pointed at a small, thin man. "I don't remember hirin' him."

"He was the last one you hired, after Fergus quit."

"Fergus quit?" Henry snapped. "When?"

"Just before we left, boss," Kent said. "Don't you remember?"

"Of course I remember!" He looked at the line. "I'm gettin' some breakfast, and then we're on our way to Maryville."

He went and accepted a plate of bacon-and-eggs from Del Brandon. Lily came up alongside Kent.

"What's wrong?" she asked.

"He's gettin' worse," Kent said.

"He's still the boss, Lyle," Lily pointed out, but she was worried that Henry was starting to get forgetful. She figured this might be the last hurrah for him and his Independence Day Gang.

In the beginning they rode through Texas, picking up children as they went along, trying not to take any who would be missed. But the last couple of rides, Henry had become less and less choosy about the kids they picked up. And although she knew they ultimately took the children to Galveston, she didn't know what Trevor Henry did with them from there. He probably sold them, but to who?

And she still didn't know what the ultimate meaning of the 4th of July was for him. Or the reason he always wanted to be in Temple City on that day.

"As long as he's got you and me, Lyle," she said, "he'll be fine."

Lyle Kent hoped Lily was right.

***

Temple City was a day's ride from Maryville. Clint arrived at dusk, passing beneath the banner that had been stretched across the street. Apparently, the Fourth of July was a huge deal in this town.

The street was quiet as darkness approached, but he was able to see decorations the townspeople had erected to celebrate the Fourth of July.

He didn't know how many hotels the town had, but the first one he saw was called The Celebration House. He reined in his horse in front. When he entered, he saw the elaborate decorations for the holiday.

"Good evening, Sir," the desk clerk greeted.

"I need a room," Clint said. "I'm hoping you're not full for the fourth."

"You're in luck. We actually have a couple of rooms left. By tomorrow we'll be full and so will the town."

"Independence Day is a big deal hereabouts, huh?"

"You know it," the man said, reversing the register book. "Sign in, please."

Clint signed his name and, for an address, he wrote Las Vegas, New Mexico.

"Here's your key, Mister . . ." The clerk looked at the register, ". . . Adams?"

"That's right."

"Uh, room eight."

"I'm going to see to my horse, and then I'll be back." He put the key in his pocket. "Thanks."

"Livery's at the end of the street."

Clint nodded his thanks and left. He untied Toby and walked the horse to the stable. He returned to the hotel with his saddlebags and rifle, found a man wearing a badge waiting in the lobby. The desk clerk hadn't wasted any time.

"Mr. Adams?" the man said. "I'm Sheriff Steve Cade. Can we talk?"

"Can we do it in my room?"

"Lead the way."

Chapter Four

Clint unlocked the door to his room and allowed the sheriff to go in ahead of him. It was a small room, but clean.

"What's on your mind, Sheriff?"

"Probably what's on every lawman's mind when the Gunsmith comes to town," Sheriff Cade responded. "What brings you here?"

"I heard your town has quite a celebration for the Fourth of July," Clint said.

"That's true."

"Well, I'm interested."

"In fireworks?"

"And whatever else your celebration includes," Clint said.

Cade studied Clint for a few moments.

"Anything else, Sheriff?"

"So you'll be here until—what? The fifth?"

"At least."

Cade nodded.

"All right, then," he said. "As long as there's no trouble . . ."

"I never look for trouble, Sheriff."

"Sure," Cade said, "it always finds you, right?"

"Well . . ."

"Enjoy our town, Mr. Adams," the man said. "I'll buy you a drink if I see you in one of our saloons."

"I'll return the favor."

Cade nodded, tossed Clint a small salute, and left. Clint felt the man might have had something else on his mind, but he would probably find out about that later. He sat on the bed a little longer, to let his tired bones rest.

***

Sheriff Cade went from the hotel to the nearby Cattleman's Club. He was shown to a table where a large, grey-haired man sat alone, sawing away at a huge steak.

"Anything for you, Sheriff?" the waiter asked.

"Just some coffee, thanks."

"What's on your mind, Sheriff?" Wayne Porter asked as the waiter walked off. The rancher didn't lift his gaze from his steak.

"Mr. Porter," Cade said, "the Gunsmith's in town."

"Clint Adams?" Porter asked, looking up from his plate. "What's he doin' here?"

"He says he came for the fireworks."

"And what do you think?"

"I think he came for the fireworks," Cade said.

"Then why tell me?"

The waiter came and set a cup of coffee down by the sheriff's elbow.

"Thanks," Cade said.

The man nodded and returned to the kitchen.

"Cade?" Porter said. "Why tell me?"

"The Independence Day Gang," Cade said.

"Jesus, that, again?" Porter said.

"There's no reason to believe they're not comin' back this year, Porter," Cade said.

"Well, then, it's your job to see that they don't do any damage," Porter said.

"We could make good use of the Gunsmith."

"How? By putting a badge on him?"

"No badge," Cade said. "But I'd make him an offer, backed by your money."

"Mine?"

"And your friends?" Cade said.

"I don't have any kids for the gang to take, Sheriff," Porter pointed out.

"Your friends do," the lawman said. "And their friends."

Porter put his knife and fork down with a bang and sat back.

"How much do you figure it'll take?" he asked.

"I don't know the man well enough to guess," Cade said, "yet. I'll be seein' him tonight."

"Are you going to get to know him enough before the Fourth?"

"We've got a few days," Cade said. "And I'm a good judge of character."

"Well then," Porter said, "when you have a number come and see me."

Cade sipped his coffee, then put the cup down and stood.

"Cade."

"Yeah?"

"You looking to hire him to protect our kids?" Porter asked.

"That, and to track down the gang and put an end to it," Cade said.

"It'd be easier to get him if he had kids of his own," Porter pointed out. "Does he?"

"No idea," Cade said. "But he's got as much of a reputation with the ladies as he has with his gun, so who knows?"

Porter leaned forward, picked up his knife and fork and said, "Find out."

Cade turned and left.

Chapter Five

Clint walked through the lobby, took a look into the hotel's dining room, then decided to take a walk and see what he could find.

It was dark, but the streets of Temple City were well lit, both by the light coming out of restaurants and saloons, and by lamp posts.

He passed several noisy establishments, but then came to a small, quiet looking café that struck his fancy. He went in, found it half empty, and got himself a table in the back.

"What can I get you, Sir?" the waiter asked. "Our menu is on the wall."

Clint looked up at a chalkboard on the wall, saw three dishes written there.

"I'll take the chicken fried steak," he said.

"Good choice, Sir. And to drink?"

"You got beer?"

"We sure do."

"A mug of cold beer."

"Comin' right up."

The beer was served in an icy mug, and the chicken fried steak was perfectly cooked.

"Anythin' else, Sir?" the waiter asked.

"No, that was plenty. Thanks."

He left the money on the table to cover the bill and stood up.

"Have you got time to answer a question or two?" Clint asked.

The waiter looked around, then said, "Sure."

"The Fourth of July," Clint said. "What's the big deal?"

"Everybody hereabouts loves the fireworks," the waiter said.

"How long has it been a big celebration?"

"A few years, now," the man said. "Everybody loves it, even with . . ."

"Even with what?" Clint prodded.

"Well . . . the kids."

"What about the kids?"

"The missing kids."

"What missing kids?" Clint asked.

The waiter looked around again. The only other customer waved at him, dropped money on the table, and left.

"Please," he said, "sit."

Clint sat back down, and the waiter sat across from him.

"Mister . . ."

"Adams," Clint said.

". . . Adams," the waiter said. "I probably shouldn't talk about this, but . . . over the past few years, on the Fourth of July, children go missing."

"Just like that?"

"They didn't just go missin'," the waiter said, "they were taken."

"By who?"

"A gang," the man said, "a gang some folks are calling The Independence Day Gang. They come by every Fourth of July, steal some kids, and move on."

"That can't be," Clint said. "If you know they're coming, they can be stopped."

"Not for, oh, about four years," the waiter said. "The sheriff has tried."

"And what do they do with the kids?"

"Who knows?" the waiter asked. "Sell 'em, maybe to Indians?"

"That's not likely," Clint said.

"Who else would buy them?" the waiter asked.

"How old are they?" Clint asked. "The missing kids?"

"Four, five, six, somethin' like that."

Clint sat and thought for a moment.

"Slavers," he said.

"What?"

"They're probably sold to slavers," Clint said, "maybe from another country."

"Who'd want little children for slaves?" the waiter asked.

"They're trainable," Clint said. "They'll grow up to be big slaves. There's a lot of money in it, or so I hear."

"How do you know so much about it?"

"I pay attention," Clint said. "What's the sheriff doing about it, this year?"

"Beats me," the waiter said, standing. "You'd have to ask him. I'm just glad I don't have any kids. I have to go back to work."

"Sure."

The waiter returned to the kitchen, and Clint left the café. He stopped just outside and looked around. It was night, which explained why there were no children around. He wondered if, when morning came, kids would be out and about, or were parents keeping them inside.

He had never heard anything about this Independence Day Gang before. He had, however, heard of slavers who captured and sold women. He had never heard of children being stolen, except by Indians, but that was in days gone by. Most Indians were now on reservations.

He decided to stop in a saloon and keep his ears open.

Chapter Six

Clint came to the Bent Axle Saloon and went inside. It was lively, tables occupied, shoulder-to-shoulder at the bar, several girls circulating on the floor. It looked like there were no house games, but there were a couple of poker games going on.

He went to the bar and elbowed his way in. It was a common occurrence, so nobody objected—not yet, anyway. Maybe later in the night, when men were drunk, it might change.

"What can I getcha?" the bartender asked.

"Beer."

The man nodded and went off to get it. Clint's plan to keep his ears open wasn't going to work. There were so many conversations going on that they mixed together into a jumble of words.

When the bartender came with the beer a voice said, "That'll be on me, Gordo."

"Sure, Sheriff."

Clint turned and saw Sheriff Cade standing behind him.

"And I'll have one," Cade said.

"Comin' up."

Cade elbowed his way in and leaned on the bar.

"So what kind of day have you had?" he asked.

"An interesting one" Clint said. "I found a small café that had a good chicken fried steak, and I heard some local gossip."

"Gossip?" Cade said, accepting the beer from Gordo. "About what?"

"Missing children," Clint said. "Or stolen children, I guess."

Cade didn't react immediately. He sipped his beer thoughtfully.

"You heard about that, huh?"

"Something called The Independence Day Gang?"

Cade made a face.

"I hate that name."

"Sounds like something a newspaper would've coined," Clint said.

"You got that right."

"How long has this been going on, Sheriff?"

"This'll be the fifth year in a row, if they come again."

"Do they only hit your town?"

"Oh no," Cade said. "They come across Texas, hitting towns, schools, churches. But every year they finish up here on the Fourth of July."

"If you know that, you should be ready for them."

"You'd think so," the sheriff said. "But they're sharp, and slippery."

"Have you ever tried to track them?"

"More than once," Cade said. "But my skills as a tracker are suspect."

"You sound like an educated man," Clint commented.

"Before I was sheriff," Cade said, "I was a schoolteacher."

"That's quite a change," Clint said. "Did you do that after the kids went missing?"

"No, no," Cade said, "well before that. Actually, it was after my wife left me because she said I was boring."

"Quite a change," Clint said.

"I ran for sheriff because the longtime peace officer was retiring. It was either me or a trigger-happy kid who thought he was Wyatt Earp."

"How long ago was that?"

"Ten years," Cade said. "The town's grown since then, and five years ago they started this Fourth of July celebration."

"And that was when the children began disappearing."

"About that time, yeah."

"Do you see any connection?"

"All I can figure is that the festivities cover up the kidnappings."

"Then why not cancel the festivities?"

"Believe me, I've recommended that, but the town fathers won't go for it."

"That sounds odd."

"What?"

"That the town 'fathers' won't do what might be best for the children."

"It's about money," Cade said. "Always about money." He finished his beer. "You want another?"

"This is my round," Clint said, and waved at the bartender for two more.

"Well," Cade said, "since you've already heard about the kids, I might as well go ahead and ask you."

"Ask me what?" Clint said, afraid of the answer.

"I'd like your help," Cade said. "The gang is coming; we all know that."

"Why not take all the children and put them in one place?" Clint asked.

"That's a lot of kids," Cade said. "And they're a big part of the Fourth of July festivities."

"Jesus," Clint said, "what's wrong with these people?"

"They won't go along with any of my suggestions," Cade said. "They feel it's my job to keep the kids safe and catch this gang."

"Do you have deputies?"

"Two," Cade said, "but they're young, and inexperienced. I need somebody I can count on."

"Are you offering me a badge?"

"No," Cade said, I'm offerin' you money. We'll pay you to work with me to bust this gang up and, hopefully, find some of these children."

"You said this happened in other towns?"

"Other towns, other counties," Cade said.

"Did you try to recruit help from those places?"

"Yes," Cade said. "They want to handle it on their own."

"But the gang is still operating."

"Up to last year," Cade said, "we had six children go missing on the Fourth."

Clint sipped his beer.

"Look," Cade said, "you stopping in town is a godsend to us. You can stop this madness."

"Me?" Clint asked. "One man against a gang of . . .how many?"

"We don't know," Cade said. "Nobody's ever seen them."

"So there could be five, ten, or a hundred."

"Yeah."

Clint sipped his beer, again.

"Look Mr. Adams," Cade said, "these are children we're talkin' about."

"You've already told me your own town is more concerned with money than with the safety of their children."

"Those are the men who run the town," Cade said, "the Mayor, the town council. I'm hoping next year we'll vote the mayor out of office. But I'm hopin' they resolve this even before then."

"Why not hire a professional tracker?"

"We tried a couple," Cade said. "They wouldn't do it."

"Why not?"

"They knew about the gang and didn't want to go up against them."

"Wait," Clint said, "they heard of this gang? Why haven't I?"

Cade shrugged.

"Maybe you weren't movin' in the same circles as the trackers."

Clint kept the lawman waiting a bit longer before replying.

"If I do this, I'll do it my way."

"Of course."

"I'll try and stop them from taking any kids this year," Clint went on."

"Okay."

"Failing that," Clint said, "I have a friend who can help me track them."

"We'll have to pay him, too?"

"Of course."

Cade sat back.

"I have to talk to some people," he said.

"Money men?"

Cade nodded.

"Then you do that and let me know," Clint said.

Cade nodded.

"I have rounds, right now," he said, standing. "Thanks for the beer. I'll get back to you tomorrow."

"I'll be here."

As the sheriff left, Clint waved at one of the girls passing by.

"I'll have another beer," he told her.

"Comin up, sweetie."

Clint watched the pretty little blonde sashay back across the room, dodging grasping hands of men along the way. She got to the bar, then made the same trip across the floor, not spilling a drop.

"Here you go, hon," she said. "Anythin' else?"

Clint studied her pretty young face, then said, "No, thanks."

"Just let me know," she said. "I'm Honey."

As she went back across the floor he muttered, "Of course you are."

Chapter Seven

July 2

The next morning Cade decided to ride out to Wayne Porter's spread, rather than wait for the man to appear at the Cattleman's Club. He gave his horse to a ranch hand and then knocked on the front door of the house. It was answered by a colored man who cared for Porter's household.

"mo'nin', Sheriff."

" 'mornin', Cyrus. Can I see the boss?"

"He havin' his breakfast now," Cyrus said. "Is it impo'tant?"

"Yes, it is," Cade said, "or I wouldn't bother him."

"I'll ask 'im, Suh."

Cyrus closed the door, returned mere moments later.

"Mr. Porter asks if you'll join him for breakfast, Sheriff?"

"I'd be happy to."

"This way."

Cyrus led him to Wayne Porter's lavish dining room, where he had been only once before, and not for a meal.

"Have a seat, Sheriff," Porter invited. "Cyrus, ask cook to bring the sheriff a plate."

"Yes, Suh."

Cade sat and watched while Porter ate his breakfast. An older woman came from the kitchen and put a plate in front of him. It was covered with a thick slice of ham, scrambled eggs, and potatoes.

"Thank you."

"My pleasure, Sheriff," she said, with a smile. "Coffee?"

"Please."

She grabbed a cup and pot from a sideboard and poured him a cup.

"That'll be all Mrs. Watson."

"Yes, sir."

She returned to the kitchen. Cyrus didn't return. Cade started to eat.

"I didn't expect to see you this soon," Porter said. He was wearing a shirt and tie, and something Cade had heard him refer to as a smoking jacket.

"I didn't expect it, either, but Adams heard about the missin' kids."

"From who?"

"That doesn't really matter."

"All right, then," Porter said. "You discussed it with him?"

"I did."

"Why?"

"He would have heard about it sooner or later."

"And?"

Cade revisited his conversation with Clint Adams to Porter, while the two men continued to eat.

"So we'll have to pay Adams and a second man?"

"That's the way it looks."

"How much?"

"He didn't say," Cade said.

"How much do you think?"

Cade stopped eating and looked at Porter.

"I think I'll need a blank check."

"A blank check?" Porter snapped. "You're crazy."

"Then you've got one other alternative, Mr. Porter," Cade said.

"Cancel the Fourth?"

"That's it."

"Can't do that."

"Then we need Adams," Cade said. "He'll either stop the gang, or he'll try to track 'em after the fact."

"With this tracker he wants to bring in?"

"Yes."

"Do we know who that is?"

"He didn't say," Cade said, "but my guess is it's somebody with a reputation like his."

"Two old time legends of the West, huh?"

"He's not that old."

"That's beside the point," Porter said. "I'll have to present this to the rest of the council."

"Of course," Cade knew the rest of them would go along with whatever Porter recommended.

"Finish your breakfast then," Porter said. "I'll ride back to town with you."

"Whatever you say."

***

Cade waited while a ranch hand hitched up Porter's buggy.

"Cade, why doesn't Adams just bring in some men and stop the gang?" Porter asked, as he climbed aboard his buggy.

"My guess is, it would take too long to round up such a group."

"All right," Porter said. "Let me see what the rest of the council has to say, and we can get him started."

"Okay."

"You take the lead, Sheriff," Porter said. "I'll keep up."

Cade rode out, with Porter's buggy following closely behind him.

Chapter Eight

Trevor Henry watched as Kent came back to camp with his two men, Hawk and Taylor, and a buckboard full of crying children.

"How many?" he asked.

"Eight," Kent said.

"Any problems?"

"It was easy," Kent said. "A whole school full of 'em."

"And the teacher?"

"We left her behind."

"Alive?"

"I think so," Kent said. "Not sure."

"Okay," Henry said. "Get these kids to Lily and tell her to shut them up."

"Right."

"Wait!" Henry said.

"Yeah?"

"You said a school full," Henry said. "How old are they?"

"Five, six, maybe seven."

"None younger?"

"No."

"We'll have to get younger ones from Temple City," he pointed out.

"Right."

"Go."

Henry watched them ride past with the kids, sipping from a coffee cup. For a moment he forgot why the kids were there.

"Shit," he said, shaking his head.

***

The morning of the second Clint rose, wondering if he was doing the right thing. He had come to Temple City to see the festivities, not to get involved with their problems. But as the sheriff had pointed out, this was about children.

He decided to stay in the hotel for breakfast and found it edible enough. When he stepped out of the hotel, he saw Sheriff Cade riding into town with a man in a buggy behind him. This was probably the man Cade was getting the money from.

Clint didn't really want money for the job, but he'd need to outfit himself and whoever he brought in to help. He had a few men in mind and would send out telegrams that morning to see who he could get.

He allowed the lawman and buggy to pass by before crossing the street.

At the telegraph office, he sent three messages out in the hopes he would reach at least one person. The clerk agreed to deliver any reply to the hotel.

Once he committed himself to the job of trying to protect the children of Temple City, he realized he had a scant two days to come up with a plan. For that he needed more information from the sheriff, so he went to the man's office.

"Come in, sit down," Cade said, when Clint entered. "I got permission to talk money with you."

"If I bring in another man, I'll need to pay him well. All I want is to outfit myself for this."

"I'll make sure you have free reign at the general store."

"I saw you ride in," Clint said. "Was that the money man with you?"

"That was Wayne Porter," Cade said. "He owns a large spread about five miles out of town. At least, that's where his house is. He has over a thousand aces."

"Impressive."

"He's behind the growth of this town," Cade said.

"Then why doesn't he cancel the Fourth of July celebration and concentrate on protecting the children?"

"Because he feels that's my job," Cade said, "and yours, now that I've recruited you."

"Okay," Clint said, "that's the part I don't understand. Why aren't local parents up in arms?"

"Porter has everyone under his thumb," Cade said. "He's convinced parents that protectin' their kids is my job."

"Does he have any children, himself?"

"No, none. No wife, either."

"Okay," Clint said, "we've got two days. I'd like to see where the children were taken from last time."

"Their homes," Cade said. "Or the area around their homes. There's no one location, like a schoolhouse or church."

"And did anyone report seeing a group of men in the area?"

"No."

Clint scratched his chin.

"And there's no guarantee they're all men," Clint added. "Most men would want to have women to take care of the children."

"That's true," Cade said, "but I hate to think that women are part of this child grabbing gang."

"I can't imagine there's a gang working in the area, without ever being seen."

"They're smart," said Cade, "and slippery."

"I guess so," Clint said. "I'll need one of your deputies to show me around."

"We can do that," Cade said, "I'll give you Johnny Reckon. He's been with me the longest."

"Fine."

"I can have him come to your hotel."

"I'll wait there."

"Sit out front," Cade suggested. "I'll have him come over there later this morning."

"Good."

Clint left the sheriff's office and headed for his hotel.

***

After Clint left, Cade grabbed his hat and gunbelt and went looking for his deputy. He found the young man eating breakfast in a café.

Cade sat down and told the deputy what he wanted to do.

"Work with the Gunsmith?" Reckon asked. "Doing what?"

"Whatever he wants you to do," Cade said. "Show him around."

"What's he lookin' for?"

"The Independence Day Gang."

Reckon's eyes widened.

"Are we gonna catch them this year?" he asked.

"I hope so, Johnny," Cade said. "I really hope so."

Chapter Nine

Clint watched as the young man wearing a badge approached the front of the hotel. He stood up.

"Deputy Johnny Reckon?" he asked.

"Yes, Sir," Reckon said.

Clint figured the man to be about twenty-five. He put his hand out and they shook.

"Good to meet you," Clint said.

"It's my pleasure, sir," Reckon said. "The sheriff says I'm to do whatever you say."

"I just want to take a look around the county," Clint said. "Maybe find a hidey-hole that this Fourth of July Gang might use."

"We can do that."

"Where's your horse?" Clint asked.

"The livery."

"Fine," Clint said, "let's start there."

***

They walked their horses out and mounted up.

"I want to stay away from the Porter ranch and all his land."

"That's gonna be hard," Reckon said. "He owns most of the land around here."

"He has no kids," Clint said. "This gang wouldn't bother with him. I want to look elsewhere."

"For a hideout?"

Clint nodded.

"A box canyon, a line shack, an arroyo, anything that a gang might use."

"I think I might know a few places," Reckon said.

"Then let's go," Clint said. "I'll follow you."

The deputy took the lead, and Clint rode behind him.

***

"Down there," Reckon said, pointing. "An arroyo. Deep enough to hide some men."

Clint stared down at it.

"No," he said, finally, "they'd have children with them, probably in wagons or buckboards. It needs to be big enough for all of that."

"There's a canyon nearby," Reckon said. "That might do it."

"Show me."

***

They rode to the canyon and Reckon waited while Clint looked it over, remaining on horseback. Eventually, he rode back to where the young deputy waited.

"What do you think?" Reckon asked.

"There's no indication that anyone ever camped here, especially not a large group."

"You can tell that even after a year?"

"There would always be some sign," Clint said.

"What now?" Reckon asked.

"I need to keep looking," Clint said. "How far are we from the Porter ranch?"

"We're skirting the border," Reckon said. "You said you wanted to avoid it."

"Can you think of any locations on the ranch?" Clint asked.

"A few."

"Far from the house?"

"Yes."

"All right," Clint said. "Show me around a bit more, and then we'll go and check those."

"We might run into some ornery ranch hands who'll wanna know what you're doin' on the property."

"Well," Clint said. "You're wearing a badge."

"Porter and his hands think they're above the law," Reckon said.

"Well then," Clint said, "I'll have to deal with them in a different way, won't I?"

***

Clint and Reckon rode the range around Temple City for most of the afternoon, and finally crossed onto the property of Wayne Porter.

It apparently didn't take long for their presence to become known.

"Here they come," Reckon said, pointing.

Clint saw five riders approaching and reined in to wait for them to issue a challenge.

"What are you two doin' on Porter land?" one of them demanded.

"This man's a deputy," Clint said. "We're here on official business. Your boss knows about it."

"He does, eh?" the man said. "He didn't tell us nothin'."

"Does your boss usually clear his decisions with you?" Clint asked. "Are you the foreman?"

"I'm top hand," the man said.

"That makes you number three," Clint said. "You better talk to Mr. Porter or your foreman before you start trouble you can't handle."

"We're startin' trouble?" the man asked, amused. He looked around at the other men, who all put their hands on their guns, tucked into their belts. The spokesman was the only one wearing a holster. Cowhands didn't usually wear guns in holsters when they were working.

"Before you men start somethin'," Reckon spoke up, "you should know this is Clint Adams."

The four men with their guns in their belts dropped their hands away from their weapons quickly. Apprehension replaced arrogance on their faces.

The man wearing the holster frowned.

"What's the Gunsmith doin' here?" he demanded.

"He's here because it's almost the Fourth of July," Reckon said.

Now the spokesman looked surprised.

"You're here because of all the missin' kids?" he asked Clint

"That's right."

"Well, why didn't ya say so?" the man asked. His shoulders relaxed and his hand fell to his side. "What can we do to help ya?"

The abrupt change in attitude surprised Clint, but he decided to take advantage of it.

"I need to know if you see any groups of men in the area," Clint said. "Also, any men leading wagons loaded with small children."

"Like settlers?" the man asked.

"But not settlers," Clint said. "The children will be stolen, and if there are also women, they'll be tending to them."

"Oh, well, yeah . . ." the man said, nodding that made sense.

"I also need to know if you men know of any areas that might be used for a campsite, or hideout."

The men all looked at each other.

"Nobody's ever asked us any of that before," the leader said.

"Well," Clint said, "we could sure cover a lot more ground if we worked together."

"You got it, Mr. Adams," the lead man said. "Where do we find ya if we see anythin'?"

"I'm at the Celebration House," Clint said. "You can find me there, or at the sheriff's office."

"Sure thing, Mr. Adams," the man said. He seemed a lot younger when he wasn't trying to be tough. "Sorry to be so aggressive with ya."

"Don't worry about it," Clint said. "You were doing your job. What's your name?"

"I'm Travis, Sir."

"All right, Travis," Clint said. "Whatever happens, I thank you for your help."

"Come on, boys," Travis said. "Let's go see what we can find."

As the five men rode away, Reckon said, "Whoa, they sure changed their tune in a hurry when they heard who you was, Clint."

"It was more the information about the kids that changed their minds."

"I guess."

"But it's not always a good idea to offer that kind of information, Johnny," Clint said. "In the future, wait for me to give my name."

"Sure, Mr. Adams," Reckon said. "I sure didn't mean no harm."

"There was no harm done," Clint said, then added, "this time."

Chapter Ten

Clint and Reckon came riding back into town late in the afternoon. They hadn't achieved much for all their riding, except to recruit some help from those cow hands.

"Whatta we do now, Mr. Adams?" Reckon asked as they came out of the livery.

"I'm going to get some supper, Johnny," Clint said. "Why don't you check in with your boss, let him know what we did—or didn't—find, and see what he wants you to do."

Reckon looked as if he would rather have been invited to supper with the Gunsmith, but he said, "Okay."

They went their separate ways, Clint to a café for supper, and the deputy to the sheriff's office.

Clint returned to the café where he'd had the chicken fried steak. It wasn't on the chalk board, this time, but there was a baked chicken dish, a steak and a pork chop.

"I think I'll have the pork chop," Clint told the waiter.

"Good choice, Sir," the waiter said. "It's glazed, you know."

"That'll be interesting," Clint said.

"And beer?"

"Yes."

"Right away, Sir."

The waiter brought the beer first.

"Not much of a suppertime crowd, eh?"

"Well," the waiter said, "there are more places to eat in town than there used to be. That's what happens when a town begins to grow. I'll get your supper, Sir."

"Thanks."

He sipped his beer while he waited, went over the day in his mind. Probably the best thing they had done was to recruit those cow hands. If anyone was going to find something it would probably be locals. Hopefully, they'd show up at the hotel with some progress.

"Here you go, Sir," the waiter said. "That's a bourbon glaze on the chop."

"Sounds good," Clint said. "Thanks."

"Mind some company?"

Clint looked at the door and saw Sheriff Cade leaning in.

"Come on in," Clint said. "Right now, it's just you and me."

Cade sat and looked at Clint's plate.

"That looks good. "What is it?"

"A bourbon-glazed pork chop."

"Sounds good."

"Waiter!"

The man appeared at the kitchen door.

"Pork chop for the law," Clint said.

"Comin' up!"

"Go ahead and eat," Cade said. "I'll talk while I wait."

Chapter Eleven

"Johnny told me about your day," Cade said. "Good thing he told those cowboys who you are."

"As it turned out, yeah," Clint said. "But I told him not to do it again."

"I understand," Cade said. "Which men did you run into?"

"We got one name," Clint said, "Travis."

"Ah, yeah," Cade said, "he's the top hand."

"Who's the foreman?"

"A man named Leo O'Neil."

"Do you think we could get Porter to commit more hands to this?" Clint asked.

"I'll have to ask him," Cade said. "But he's all about money. Committing his hands to a search will cost him money. At least, that's the way he'll see it."

"He's committing money to me, isn't he?" Clint asked.

"That's not all his money," Cade said. "Some of it's the towns."

"I think I better meet this Wayne Porter," Clint said.

"What do you think you'll accomplish?" the sheriff asked as the waiter brought out his plate.

"It'll help me decide how much to charge him."

***

After supper Clint and Sheriff Cade left the café together.

"You really want to meet Porter?" Cade asked.

"I do."

"He'd be eating his supper at the Cattleman's Club," Cade said.

"Lead the way."

Cade led Clint halfway across town to a large, two-story building. There was a dark-clad man wearing a gun, standing at the front door.

"Sheriff," he said. "Here to see Mr. Porter?"

"That's right."

"He said to let you in," the man said. Then he looked at Clint. "Who's this?"

"Clint Adams," Cade said. "He's with me."

"I dunno . . ." the man said.

"Mr. Porter's expecting him."

"Well, all right," the man said. "If you say so."

He opened the door and allowed both men to enter.

"He's not the foreman, is he?" Clint asked.

"No," Cade said, "just a fella Porter hired to watch the door."

Inside the club a man in a tuxedo greeted them and led them to a dining room. Several men were seated at tables in pairs and threes, but one man was seated alone.

"That's got to be him," Clint said.

"Yep."

They crossed the room and reached Porter's table. The man looked up at him. Clint figured him for the wrong side of fifty, but aging well.

"Sheriff," Porter said, looking up from his steak. "This must be Mr. Adams."

"That's right," Clint said.

"Please, sit," the rancher invited. "Have you eaten?"

"We have," Cade said, as the two men sat.

"Do you mind if I continue while you tell me what's on your mind?"

"Not at all."

"This isn't about canceling the Fourth, is it?" Porter asked. "We've discussed that, already."

"I admit I don't understand celebrating while children are being kidnapped, but that's not why I'm here," Clint said. "A deputy and I ran into some of your men on your ranch today."

"I hope they didn't give you a hard time."

"They were about to, but when we told them why we were there, they offered to help, instead."

"My boys are good boys," Porter said.

"That's the impression I got," Clint said. "That's why I wanted to ask if you'd commit more men to our cause."

"How many did you get today?"

"Five."

"That should be enough," Porter said. "Any more than that would cost me money."

"That's what the sheriff thought you'd say," Clint told him.

"The sheriff's a smart man."

"So I can't convince you to give us more?" Clint asked.

"Mr. Adams," Porter said, "you're going to be paid for your services. Why don't you just let my men do what they're being paid to do?"

"All right," Clint said, "then let's talk about payment."

Porter put his utensils down, as if this was the important part of the conversation.

"The sheriff told me he wanted a blank check for your services."

Clint looked at Cade in surprise.

"I didn't mention that because I never thought I'd get it," Cade explained.

"Well, you have it," Porter said. "I've talked with the other members of the council, and they've agreed."

"Then there's nothing else to discuss," Clint said, standing. Clint added to Porter, "This is going to cost you big," and left.

Chapter Twelve

Trevor Henry sat with Lily and Kent as they ate their dinner away from the other men in camp.

"Who's watching those kids?" Henry asked Lily.

"Gregory, while I'm eatin'."

Henry didn't remember who Gregory was, but he kept that to himself.

"I don't hear them," he said.

"He keeps them pretty quiet," Lily said. "He's young, so the kids accept him as one of them."

"How young?"

"Fifteen."

"What is he doin' here?" Henry asked. "We deal in tykes."

Lily looked at Kent. They both remembered when Henry agreed to let them bring him on.

"He agreed to come with us and look after the children," Lily said. "And I could use the help."

"Yeah, okay," Henry groused. He didn't remember that, but he trusted Lily.

"Tomorrow's the third," Kent said. "We could hit Temple City then."

"We hit them on the Fourth," Henry said.

"So we waste tomorrow, just sittin' around?" Kent asked. "They wouldn't expect us on the third."

"Look," Henry said, "our system has been workin' for years. I don't wanna mess with it. We hit Temple City on the Fourth, like always."

Kent looked at Lily, who turned her head.

"They're gonna be waitin' for us, boss," Kent said.

"That sheriff has to act alone," Henry said. "Or with the two nobody deputies he has."

"What if the town has hired more help?"

Henry laughed.

"Not that town," he said. "They're all about money. And they're gettin' bigger."

"Then why don't we just rob the bank?" Kent asked.

Henry stopped eating his beans-and-bacon and stared at the man.

"I'm not a bank robber, Lyle!"

"You're a kidnapper, but you won't rob a bank?" Kent asked.

"I'm not a kidnapper, either," Henry said. "I'm a slaver."

"What's the difference?"

"Slavers have been around for centuries," Henry said. "It's a noble profession."

Kent and Lily exchanged a glance as Henry went back to eating.

***

"Was that what you expected?" Clint asked, as they left the club.

"Exactly," Cade said, "except for the blank check."

"Will he abide by that?" Clint asked. "No matter how much I ask for in the end?"

"I really don't know," Cade said. "I've always known him to stand by his word, but he also does what'd suit him the best."

"Then I'm surprised he's letting us keep the five men we have."

"We'll see how long he does that," Cade commented. "Look, I've got rounds to make."

"Why not let a deputy do it?"

"I'm taking one with me," Cade said. "Why don't I meet you later in the Bent Axle Saloon?"

"Fine," Clint said. "Maybe we'd have heard from Porter's cowboys by then. We can buy them a drink."

"See you there in a couple of hours," Cade said, and they went their own ways.

Chapter Thirteen

Clint relaxed at the Bent Axle bar for a while. He had stopped at the hotel first, but there were no messages from the cowboys.

"You're back."

He turned and saw the cute blonde saloon girl.

"I'm back."

"Want a table?" she asked.

"I think I'll stand here a while," he told her.

"Well," she said, "it's busy as hell, but if you decide you want a table, I'll get you one."

"Thanks."

"Do you remember my name?" she asked.

"How could I forget," he said, "Honey."

"Very good," she complimented him. "I'll see you later."

He watched her flounce away into a crowd of grasping hands.

At that moment the batwing doors exploded inward, and five men entered. They spotted Clint and hurried to the bar.

"The sheriff said you're buyin'," Travis said.

"I am," Clint said. "What'll you have?"

"Beers, all around."

"Five beers," Clint called to the bartender.

When all five men had a mug of beer, they turned to face Clint.

"Thanks, Mr. Adams," Travis said.

"You're welcome."

All six of them drank, and then Clint asked, "Did you find anything?"

"We found a couple of locations that could be likely hideouts."

"Are they all on Porter property?"

"They are," Travis said. "We can show you tomorrow."

"Well, we've got all day," Clint said. "If the Fourth comes and we haven't found them, we'll be in trouble."

"What happens then?" Travis asked.

"I'll have to track them after the fact," Clint said.

"Won't that be easier?" one of the other men asked. "I mean, with all them kids in tow, they'll leave an easy trail."

"If that was true, they would've been found by now," Clint suggested. "I'd prefer to stop them before they grab any more kids. For that we have to find them even before they get here."

"Huh?" one of the cowboys said.

"That makes no sense," another said.

"I get what he means," Travis said. "Don't worry, Mr. Adams, we'll show you them spots tomorrow."

"Thanks, Travis. Where can we meet?"

"Same place we ran into you today," Travis said. "We can go from there."

"Good," Clint said. "I'll be there. Meanwhile, let me get you boys another beer . . ."

***

After a second beer Clint took Honey up on her offer of a table, only it was for all six of them. They sat around the table, drank and laughed, until Clint finally decided it was time for him—the older of the group—to turn in.

"Don't stay here too much longer," he advised, as he stood. "We have to meet early tomorrow."

"Don't worry, Clint," Travis said. "We'll be there."

Honey hooked her arm into Clint's and walked him to the batwing doors.

"They're not drinkin' on you all night, are they?" she asked.

"Nope," he said. "I'm done. They're on their own, now."

"I just wanted to make sure," she said. " 'night, sweetie."

He went out the doors and directly to his hotel.

***

The next morning he had breakfast at the hotel, then saddled up at the livery and rode out to where he and Johnny Reckon had met up with the cowboys the day before. When he arrived, he found not five of them waiting for him, but one, Travis.

" 'mornin', Travis," he said. "Where are the others?"

"Well, they drank a might too much last night, Mr. Adams," Travis said. When drunk the night before he had started calling him "Clint," but today he was back to being respectful. "But I'm here and I can show ya what we found."

"Let's go, then."

Travis took the lead and spent the rest of the morning showing Clint a few places he and his friends had picked out as likely hideouts for a gang.

After they had seen three, Travis asked Clint, "So, whataya think, Mr. Adams?"

"Well," Clint said, "one place was an old line shack, too small for any kind of gang."

"But hidden away," Travis said.

"Another was a canyon that's been overgrown and not stepped foot in for years."

"So they ain't used it, but they might, this time," Travis said.

"And another spot was just too damned small for any use," Clint said. "Travis, I appreciate what you and your partners did, but I'm afraid it hasn't really been any help."

"Well," Travis said, scratching his head, "I dunno what else I can do, Mr. Adams. The boss told me I could spend the mornin' with ya, but I gotta get back to work."

"The boss? Mr. Porter?"

"No, Sir," Travis said, "Leo O'Neil, the foreman."

"Ah," Clint said, "and he gets his orders from Mr. Porter."

"Well, yessir."

"Tell me something, Travis," Clint said. "Why would Mr. Porter not want to do anything to help these missing children? Or to keep any other children from behind taken?"

"I dunno, Mr. Adams," Travis said. "I guess he should want to."

"Yes, he should," Clint said. "It just seemed to me he doesn't care."

"I dunno . . ." Travis said. "But I gotta get back to work, Mr. Adams."

"Well, you do that, Travis," Clint said. "You go back to work, and tell your partners I appreciate all you and them tried to do."

"I wish we could do more," Travis said. "I surely do."

"I know you do, Travis," Clint said. "I know you do."

Clint watched the young cowboy ride back toward the ranch, then turned his horse and rode back to town.

Chapter Fourteen

Upon arriving in town, Clint left his horse at the livery and went to his hotel. There the clerk handed him three telegrams. He took them with him to his room.

One was from his friend Talbot Roper's office. Roper was the best private detective in the country, with an office in Denver. Apparently, he had a girl reading his mail, as she had sent Clint a telegram telling him that Roper was out of town on a case.

The second telegram was from John Locke, in New Mexico. Also known as The Widowmaker, Locke said he was due in Washington on some kind of matter he would find out the details of when he got there. He said he'd keep in touch so Clint would know where he was, and if he found that he really needed him, he'd be there.

The third telegram was from Kit Boone, a descendant of the famous Daniel Boone. Clint had rarely, if ever, asked Boone for help, but the man was probably the best tracker he had ever known. And while it was true that a man leading wagons full of children probably wouldn't be hard to find, the question remained why had he not yet been tracked?

Boone said he was on his way, no questions asked.

He had asked Locke and Roper for help many times. They knew they could turn him down with good excuses, and there'd be no hard feelings. Since Clint had not been in contact with Boone for a long time, the man probably felt compelled to reply that he was on his way. Clint was glad he'd be able to pay Boone very well, compliments of Temple City's blank check.

If Wayne Porter had any intention of not coming through on that check, Clint would take it out of his hide.

Clint was satisfied by the three replies he had received.

His stomach was growling. He decided to have lunch, and then check in with the sheriff. He went back to the café he had now chosen to have most of his meals in. Their lunch menu was also three items on a chalkboard, so he chose one at random, fairly certain it would be good.

The waiter brought him a meat loaf sandwich with a variety of vegetables on the side, and a beer.

"It's nice to have a regular customer, for a change," the man said.

"I'll eat here as long as I'm in town," Clint promised.

"Take yer time, friend," the waiter said. "I got all day."

Clint ate his lunch and told the man he would be back for supper. Then he left and went to the sheriff's office.

***

When he walked in Cade looked up from his desk and smiled.

"Afternoon," the man said. "Find anything?"

"Not a damned thing," Clint said, "and I lost those five cowboys."

"Lost them?"

"Porter pulled them all back to go to work."

Cade sat back in his chair.

"That doesn't surprise me."

"It still makes me wonder why that man doesn't want to protect your town's children."

"I just don't think he wants to do anything that will cut into his profits," Cade said.

"And the people in this town accept that from a member of their town council?" Clint asked. "What about your mayor?"

"He's just a mouthpiece for Porter," Cade said. "The council runs the town, and Porter runs the council."

"So, you work for Wayne Porter?"

"Essentially, yes, if I want to keep this job."

"Which you do."

"Yes," Cade said, "at least until a better one comes along."

"Can't say I blame you for that," Clint relented, dropping into a chair.

"What are you going to do now?"

"I'm not done looking for a likely hideout," Clint said. "I'll just have to do it alone."

"You can still have Johnny."

"I might take you up on that."

"What happens if you can't stop them this time?" Cade asked.

"Then I change direction. I'll have to track them."

"And you got help for that?"

"I do," Clint said. "An expert tracker."

"And you think you'll need an expert for that?" Cade asked. "To track a gang hauling kids in wagons?"

"Well, you never found them."

Cade laughed.

"I told you," he said. "Before this job I was a school-teacher. I know nothing about tracking. But I thought you did."

"I do," Clint said, "but this gang's been operating for . . . what? Five years? And nobody's tracked them? I think I'll take all the help I can get."

"And when does this help arrive?"

"Probably tomorrow." Clint stood. "You know what? Have Johnny meet me at my hotel with his horse, and we'll get back out there."

"Will do."

Clint nodded and left the office.

Chapter Fifteen

Johnny Reckon was waiting in front of the hotel when Clint walked over with Toby.

"Where to today, Mr. Adams?" he asked.

"We're going to ride east of town, away from the Porter spread."

"But in the past, everybody says they come from the west," Johnny said.

"After a few years of it, they'll probably know that we're waiting for them," Clint said. "They might be changing their strategy."

"Then they might come from the north or the south," Reckon offered.

"We'll look there, too," Clint said. "It's going to be a long day.

And it was.

***

Wayne Porter looked up when his foreman brought Travis into his office.

"Thanks, O'Neil," Porter said. "That's all."

"Yessir."

"Sit down, Travis," Porter said.

"Yessir," the young cowboy said.

"What'd you tell Clint Adams when you saw him?" Porter asked.

"Just what O'Neil tol' me to tell 'im, Sir," Travis said. "We gotta go back to work and can't help him no more."

"Did you show him the places you picked out?"

"Yessir."

"And?"

"He wasn't impressed."

"So he still has nothing."

"No sir," Travis said. "I mean, yessir, he's got nothin'."

"All right, then," Porter said. "That's all. Send O'Neil back in."

"Yessir."

Travis left and the foreman reappeared.

"Leo," Porter said, "I want you to keep the men working, keep them out of town, away from Clint Adams. Understood?"

"Yessir."

"That's all."

The foreman nodded and backed out.

Porter directed his attention back to the work on his desk. Work that would bring him a considerable profit.

***

After spending most of the day on horseback, Clint and Johnny Reckon rode back into town, their tired asses aching almost as much as their horses were.

They stopped in front of the sheriff's office, and the man came out.

"You fellas look beat all to hell and back," Sheriff Cade commented.

"We're more than just beat," Clint said.

"Plumb wore out," Reckon added.

"Do you have anything to show for it, at least?" Cade asked.

"I'll meet up with you in the Axle later and I'll tell you how our day went," Clint said. "We want a bath and a meal before anything else."

"I guess you deserve them," Cade said. "I'll see you boys later."

As they rode from the sheriff's office to the livery, Reckon said, "The sheriff ain't gonna be happy with what we have, Clint."

"That'll just make two of us," Clint said.

***

Clint took Johnny Reckon with him to the café, where they both had huge steaks. Then they split up. Clint went to the hotel for a bath. He didn't know what Reckon did. The deputy wasn't talking about a bath as much as Clint had been on the way back.

Clint had his bath, which he soaked in for a spell, then dressed in clean clothes.

When he went back down to the lobby, the desk clerk waved him over.

"Another telegram, Sir."

"Thanks."

He opened it there in the lobby and read it. Kit Boone assured him he would be in Temple City on the Fourth of July. That suited Clint. He folded the telegram and tucked it in his shirt pocket. At least he knew he'd have one man he trusted backing his play.

He left the hotel and walked to the Bent Axle, which was as alive with action as ever. He was depending on Honey to get him a table, again.

Chapter Sixteen

Clint found he arrived at the Axle before the sheriff. He got a beer from the bar, then turned to see Honey approaching him.

"Are you gonna want a table for tonight?" she asked him.

"I am," he said, "for me and the sheriff."

"I got one for you in the back," she said. "And I'll watch for the sheriff."

"I appreciate that."

He followed her to the table and then watched her twitching butt walk away from him.

She brought him a second beer and, moments later, lead the sheriff over to his table, carrying a beer for the lawman.

"Thanks, Honey," Clint said.

Cade sat and said, "Looks like you made a friend."

"She and the waiter at the café are very happy with me," Clint admitted.

Cade picked up his beer and drank from it.

"You were going to tell me what you accomplished today," he said to Clint.

"Nothing," Clint said. "Absolutely nothing."

"That was the feeling I got."

"Oh, we found some locations that might make good hideouts for a gang, but not a gang hauling stolen children. I can't imagine where they're going to camp, what with the children they already have, and the ones they plan to kidnap from here."

"So we'll have to wait for them to make their move."

"I guess so."

"This town will be hopping tomorrow," Cade said. "There's a fireworks display after dark, but I'm sure there'll be some going on during the day. Plus there's a Fourth of July picnic for the whole town."

"Where's that?"

"In a field at the southern end of town."

"And there'll be kids there."

"Undoubtedly."

"So those kids will be safe," Clint suggested.

"I'd say so."

"Then where will the gang be getting their victims from?" Clint asked.

"From kids who aren't at the picnic, I'd guess."

"Won't most of the parents here abouts be taking their kids to the picnic?" Clint asked.

"I'm sure there are ranchers with kids who'll be staying home for their own celebrations," Cade commented.

"It seems to me parents would do anything to keep their kids safe," Clint said.

"You'd think that would be the case," Cade said.

"Well," Clint said, "it's frustrating to try and help people who won't help themselves."

Cade finished his beer and stood up.

"I'm sorry Johnny wasn't more help to you."

"He was fine," Clint said. "I think he'll be a good deputy for you."

"I agree," Cade said. "Well, I'd better get ready for tomorrow."

"Ready for the celebration?"

Cade looked Clint in the eye and said, "Ready for anything."

***

After Cade left, Clint had another beer and watched the activity in the saloon. People seemed very happy. There was a lot of talk about the Fourth, but Clint couldn't detect any talk of kidnapped children.

"Another beer?" Honey asked, sidling up alongside him.

"I think I'll finish this one and turn in," he told her. "Thanks just the same."

"Is there anything else I can do for you?"

He stared at her sweet young face, long blonde hair and flawless skin. But before he could think of a proper response she spoke again.

"What hotel are you at?" she asked.

"The Celebration."

"Ah, that's a good place," she said. "Tell me, do you always lock your room door?"

"Always," he said.

"That's a pity," she said, then turned and hurried away.

Sweet girl.

***

Clint returned to his room, locked the door, hung his gunbelt on the bedpost, then sat on the bed and removed his boots. Before he could get any further someone jiggled his doorknob, then knocked. He took his gun from his holster and carried it to the door.

"Yes?"

"It's Honey," a soft voice said.

He cracked the door, saw Honey in the hallway, wearing a shawl over her naked, creamy shoulders.

"You really do lock your door," she said to him.

Chapter Seventeen

Honey entered the room and removed her shawl. Clint could feel the heat emanating from her body.

"I've never been in one of these rooms before," she said, looking around. "It's small."

"But clean," Clint said, "and comfortable enough." He walked to the bedpost and holstered his gun, then turned. "What brings you here, Honey?"

"I wanted to see if you locked your door," she said, walking around the room.

"Why?"

"I was going to sneak in," she said.

"And?"

She smiled and turned to face him.

"And crawl into bed with you," she said. "I thought you might know that and keep the door unlocked."

"I never keep my door unlocked," he said, "for any reason."

"But you *were* expecting me, weren't you?"

"Well . . ."

"I thought you wanted me to come."

"Are you here because it's your job?" he asked.

"Oh, no," she said. "My job is in the saloon. When I leave there, I'm on my own time."

"Then why are you here?" he asked.

"Oh, you know," she said, coming closer. She put her arms around his neck. "I'm here for you."

She kissed him, then, gently at first, then more firmly. It went on for some time, long enough for him to lean in and help. Then she drew back and looked at him.

"That was nice," she said.

"Yes, it was."

"Let's do it again."

"One minute," he said, disentangling himself from her arms.

He walked to the door and made sure it was locked, then took a wooden chair and jammed the back beneath the door to make sure.

She went to the bed and sat.

"Hmm, you want to keep me in, don't you?"

"On the contrary," he said, "I'm keeping other people out."

"What other people?"

He shrugged.

"Who knows?"

"Do you think someone sent me here?"

"Again," he said, "who knows?"

She laughed.

"Nobody sent me," she said. "I came here to sleep with you, pure and simple."

"Why me?" he asked. "Why not one of the younger men in the saloon?"

"Young men are boring," she said. "They don't know what they're doing."

"I see. And old men?"

"They know what to do, but they're too tired to do it," she said, laughing. "Now you, you're just the right age."

He studied her a moment. She couldn't have been more than twenty-five, with a body that was full and firm.

"What are you thinking now?" she asked.

"That it's time to stop talking," he said.

"Oh, yes!" she said.

She stood up, reached behind her, undid the back of her dress and then shrugged. The dress fell to the floor, revealing her body in all its golden glory. The bush between her legs was as luminous as the hair on her head. Her pale skin seemed to have a golden hue, her large, round breasts tipped with pink nipples.

"And now you, Sir," she said.

Quickly, Clint got rid of his clothes, and when his hard cock came into view, she stared at it hungrily.

"Still think someone sent me?" she asked, with a smile.

"It doesn't matter," he said. "I'm going to shoot anyone who comes through that door."

He walked to her and gathered her into his arms while she laughed . . .

***

Trevor Henry looked up as a man entered the barn. His men were around him, and the children were huddled in a corner.

"The boss wants to see you," he said.

"Lead the way," Henry said. "Kent! I'll be back in a minute."

"Yeah, sure."

"Make sure Lily keeps those brats quiet."

Kent nodded.

Henry turned and followed the man out and to the big house.

Inside he found Wayne Porter waiting for him, sitting at his desk in his office.

"Trevor!" Porter said. "Good to see you. Can I get you a drink?"

"Not if it's that brandy stuff you drink," Henry said.

"I've got whiskey."

"I'll take it."

"Have a seat." Porter walked to a sideboard loaded with bottles and poured Henry a whiskey. He walked back to the desk and handed it to him, then sat down again.

"How are things going?" he asked.

"We're right on target," Henry said. "We'll make a big haul tomorrow, and then head out."

"That sounds good," Porter said. He picked up his brandy glass and held it up. "Happy Fourth."

"Not for some," Trevor Henry said, and drank.

***

When Henry walked back into the big barn Lyle Kent asked, "What'd he want?"

"Just checkin' to see if we're on schedule."

"You told him we are, right?"

"Of course I told him that," Henry said, "because we are, right?"

"We're here," Kent said, "and tomorrow's the Fourth."

"Then let's make sure the job gets done," Henry said. "You got it?"

"I got it, Trevor."

At that moment a child cried out.

"Go and tell Lily to shut that brat up!" Henry said, his head suddenly throbbing.

Chapter Eighteen

After spending a short time with Trevor Henry, Wayne Porter was sure something was wrong with the man. He seemed . . . scattered, not the man Porter had hired five years before to run these raids. He was starting to think it might be time to find somebody else. That would mean getting rid of Trevor Henry. He wondered if Lyle Kent would be able to do both those jobs, or if he'd have to hire somebody entirely new?

He poured himself another brandy, then looked down at the paperwork on his desk. This next haul was going to bring him a big profit. He needed Trevor Henry to keep it together long enough to get these kids to Galveston and delivered to that ship.

"Boss?"

He looked up and saw the foreman, Leo O'Neil, standing in the doorway.

"Yeah, Leo?"

"You need me for anythin' else?"

"Just make sure Henry and his people get what they need," Porter said.

"Yessir, I will."

"Good man. That's all."

As O'Neil walked away, Porter wondered if the foreman might be a likely replacement?

***

Honey may have been young, but she was very knowledgeable about not only her body, but Clint's, as well. He didn't know if she was a whore as well as a saloon girl, but it didn't matter.

He was anxious to explore her body, so full of curves and shadow. But she was much more anxious to roam his body, so he just laid back and let her have at it.

She covered him with kisses, rubbed her body against his, shimmied down between his legs and licked his cock til it was good and wet, and then sucked it into her mouth with great relish. She sucked him avidly, moaning her pleasure, bringing him to the brink of completion before letting him slide free and smiling up at him.

"Not yet, Mister," she said, "not yet."

She slid up on him and took the length of him into her hot, wet pussy. Literally jumping up and down on him, she let her head loll back on her neck and groaned aloud each time she came down.

She was enjoying herself immensely, and he liked watching her large breasts bob up and down as she rode him. He found her rhythm and matched it, reaching out to hold her by the hips. But eventually he wasn't able to resist any longer, and reached up to hold her breasts, thumbing the hard nipples as he did. She bit her lips and looked down at him.

"Pinch 'em," she told him, urgently, "come on, pinch 'em hard!"

He obeyed, taking each of her lovely nipples between his thumb and forefinger and pinching them. Her eyes went wide and she cried out her approval. She bounced and laughed and moaned until he finally erupted inside of her, and her insides seemed to milk every drop from him like a hot, wet, grasping hand . . .

***

Moments later she was on her back next to him, breathing heavily. She reached out her left hand and held his semi-hard penis.

"That was nice," he said.

"That was a good start," she corrected, stroking him. As he got harder, she said, "My God, I see you're already lookin' for more!"

Chapter Nineteen

Clint took his turn, moving his hands and mouth over her bountiful body until she was begging him to "stick it in!"

Instead, he settled down between her thighs and worked on her with his tongue until she was writhing and holding back screams. Only then did he mount her and stick it in driving in and out of her until he, once again, exploded . . .

***

"Omigod!" she said, covering her face with her hands as she once again settled onto her back. "You're tryin' to kill me with pleasure."

"Can you think of a better way to do it?"

"I've never been with a man before who knows what a woman wants, like you do."

"I've had some practice," he said.

"I bet you have."

"You pretty much know what you're doing, yourself," he told her.

"I guess we've both had practice," she said, then added, "not that I'm a whore."

"I never thought you were," he lied.

"You're sweet to lie," she said. "All men think saloon girls are also whores."

"What you do and who you do it with is your business," he said.

"I take my pleasure where I can," she said, "and I've never taken money for it."

"That makes two of us," he said. "I've never paid for it."

"A man with your skills doesn't have to pay," she said, "ever!"

She sat up and swung her feet to the floor.

"Are you leaving?" he asked.

"I have to," she said. "If I stay any longer, I won't be able to walk tomorrow."

He watched as she put her dress back on.

"What will you be doin' tomorrow for the Fourth?" she asked.

"I have some business," he said.

"So you won't be at the big town picnic?"

"You never know," he said. "I might."

"Well," she said, "if you're there, I'll see you."

She came to the bed and kissed him goodnight. After she left, he got up and locked the door, again, then went to sleep.

***

In the morning he knew what Honey had meant by not being able to walk. His legs were weak from his night with her. If she had stayed any longer, neither of them would have been able to walk the next morning.

But in addition to his legs being weak, his stomach was also grumbling. He got dressed and walked to his preferred café. The waiter smiled when he came into the empty place.

" 'mornin', Sir. I was wonderin' if you'd come in today."

"Why wouldn't I?" Clint asked.

"I dunno," the waiter admitted. "It's the Fourth, everybody's waitin' for the big picnic."

Clint sat and asked, "You won't be at the picnic?"

"I wasn't invited."

"I've never asked you this, but do you own this place?"

"I do," the man said. "I'm the waiter, the cook, and the cleaner."

"Well, I don't know if I'll be making it to the picnic at all," Clint said, "So I'd like a big breakfast, and I'll probably be back for supper."

"Suits me, Sir," the man said. "I'll get your breakfast. And if you'll allow me, I'll make it special."

"Go ahead, then," Clint said. "Surprise me."

Clint ended up with a table full of food, including eggs, spuds, steak, bacon, flapjacks and biscuits. By the time he was finished, he didn't know if he would be able to eat supper later.

"How was it?" the waiter asked.

"It was great," Clint said. "The steak and bacon together was one of the best things I've ever had."

"I wish I didn't hafta charge ya," the man said, "but you're my only customer."

"I'm happy to pay you," Clint said, handing over the money. "What's your name, anyway?"

"Aw, just call me Cookie. That's what they called me in the army."

"Do you think you'd attract more customers if you had a sign up? What's the name of the place?"

"Ain't got a name," Cookie said. "Not yet, anyway. I only opened a coupla months ago."

"Well, take my word for it," Clint said. "A name would help. How about Cookie's Place?"

"That'll be it!" the man said, happily. "I'll have it painted on."

"I hope it brings you business," Clint said, on his way out. "You deserve it."

Chapter Twenty

Great sex and a good breakfast—or even the other way around—had taken Clint's mind off the task he had agreed to. As he stepped from the café, he saw the street was alive with activity. Firecrackers were already being set off, and children were running in the street. As a group of them went by, he saw that they were probably aged from eight to twelve. He tried to recall if anyone had told him the ages of the missing children. It seemed to him someone had mentioned five or six years olds. That meant these children were hopefully safe.

But if the eight to twelve year olds were on the streets, and attending the picnic, where were the younger children?

Clint crossed the street and walked along, still observing the festivities. Storekeepers had decorated their windows, some hadn't opened, probably planning to attend what would be a day long holiday picnic. Some people rushed past Clint, others simply walked by and nodded to him. He saw some mothers holding tightly to the hands of their children. It seemed people were concerned for the safety of their children.

As he walked, Clint saw the sheriff coming toward him from the other direction.

"Up and about, huh?" Cade asked. "Had breakfast?"

"Oh, yeah," Clint said, "enough to last me a life-time."

"So what's next?"

"There seems to be a lot of kids in town."

"They're here for the picnic and the fireworks," Cade said.

"Where are the small kids?" Clint asked. "The—what would you call them—toddlers?"

"Toddlers," Cade said, "yes, that's the age group that's been grabbed over the past few years."

"They must be taking them to sell."

"But where?" Cade wondered. "Sell them where?"

"Well, someplace to put them on the market."

"Market?"

"Slave market."

"Slave market?" Cade said, surprised. "I thought they'd be selling them to the Indians."

"Maybe ten years ago," Clint said, "but while the Indians are on the reservations, they're not buying white children."

"Then where are they selling them?" Cade asked.

Clint thought a moment, then said, "Overseas."

"What?"

"Yeah," Clint said, "there are still slave markets overseas."

"Then how do they get them there?"

"By ship," Clint said.

"So they have to get them to a port," Cade said. "Where? San Francisco? They're always shanghaiing people there."

"San Francisco's too far to travel with all those kids in a wagon or a buckboard," Clint said. "The same thing's true of New York."

"So where?" Cade asked.

"I don't know," Clint said. "I'm thinking if I get there before they do, I can stop them."

"You mean, instead of tracking them?"

Clint nodded.

"Even if you thought you knew where they were going, that'd be a risk, Clint."

"I know it," Clint said. "I'm just trying to figure out what to do next."

"Well, I've got Johnny ready to be with you today. I mean, as soon as you figure out what you're doing."

"Good, that's good," Clint said. "Let's go get him."

"He's at the office," Cade said. "Let's go."

***

When Wayne Porter walked into the barn, Trevor Henry was surprised. Porter usually stayed away from the rest of Henry's crew, and the kids.

"Henry? A word."

"We're packing up to go, Mr. Porter," Henry said, as they walked outside.

"I only need a minute."

They left the barn and walked to the end of the corral.

"What's on your mind?"

"Galveston," Porter said. "I need you to skip the last two stops you usually make and head for Galveston. You've got to get this load on that ship."

"That was always the plan," Henry said.

"Well, I got a telegram this morning," Porter said. "You need to be there by the fifteenth."

"That's eleven days," Henry said. "With these wag-onloads of kids, that's a two-week trip."

"You've got ten days," Porter said. "If you don't get this load to Galveston by then, you don't get paid."

"What?"

"That's it," Porter said. "Get going."

"Porter," Henry said, "we have to skip Temple City and head for Galveston now."

"Today's the Fourth," Porter said. "Stick to the plan and head for Galveston tomorrow."

"And get there in ten days?"

"That's the plan," Porter said. "I trust you're the man who can get it done."

Trevor Henry watched Porter walk to the house, then turned to go back into the barn.

Chapter Twenty-One

Johnny Reckon was sitting at Cade's desk when he and Clint walked in.

"Trying it on for size, Johnny?" Clint asked.

Reckon jumped up.

"Sorry, Sheriff!"

"Never mind, Johnny," Cade said. "I'm giving you to Clint for the day."

"That's fine with me, Sheriff," Reckon said. "What're we doin' today, Clint?"

"What we've been doing," Clint said. "We're going to try and head off that gang of child kidnappers."

"We ain't been so lucky, so far," Reckon said.

"Don't I know it," Clint said. "Thanks, Sheriff. I'll return Johnny unharmed."

"In one piece'll do."

Clint and Reckon left the office and stopped just outside.

"Where to?"

"Let's get our horses while I think that one over," Clint said.

***

Once they had their horses Clint asked Reckon to take him to the site of the big picnic. It was in a clearing just outside of town, and when they got there Clint saw the rows of tables, covered with red-and-white checked tablecloths. There was a group of women getting the food laid out, as the picnic was scheduled to start any time. There were men still erecting tables and benches.

"Makes me hungry just watchin'," Reckon said.

"I don't know if we'll have time to eat," Clint said. "We've got to look for that gang."

"But there's gonna be fried chicken," Reckon said.

"I'll try and get you back in time to have a leg," Clint promised.

"I like the breast," Reckon said.

"I'll get you two," Clint said. "Do you know all these people?"

"Most of 'em," Reckon said.

"Do they have children?"

"A lot of them do."

"What ages?" Clint asked.

"All ages."

"Johnny," Clint said, "who's got the biggest family in town?"

"That'd be Hurd and Lee Hatfield. They got nine kids."

"Are any of them here?" Clint asked.

Reckon stood in his stirrups and looked around.

"I don't see 'em," the deputy said.

"Take me their house, Johnny," Clint said, "and let's do it fast."

***

Johnny Reckon led the way at a gallop to the Hatfield home. It looked like a small house for a husband-and-wife with nine children. The barn was in need of paint and repair.

"This is it?" Clint asked.

"Yep."

"Where is everybody?"

"Who knows?" Reckon asked.

"Well, they're not at the picnic site."

"They could be in town," Reckon said. "Shoppin', or somethin'."

"What does Hatfield do?" Clint asked.

"Whatever he can," Reckon said, "The man's got nine kids. He does carpentry, odd jobs, whatever he can."

"Carpentry?" Clint asked. "This place looks like it can use a carpenter."

"Yeah, but nobody'd be payin' him to work on his own place."

"Let's check the house and barn," Clint said.

Both were empty but had recently been occupied.

"How old are the kids?" Clint asked.

"Oh, I dunno," Reckon said. "The oldest must be fifteen, the youngest ain't even walkin', yet."

Clint eyed the ground between the house and barn.

"I don't see that any riders have been here," he said.

"You're worried the kids've been taken?"

"Some of them would be the right age," Clint said. "But if they were taken, they weren't taken from here. Let's see if they're in town."

"They could be at the picnic by now," Reckon said.

"Yeah," Clint said. "We'll check there, too."

***

They didn't find the Hatfield family in town, so they rode out to the picnic site, again. Folks had started eating. There were also children running around the area.

"See them?" Clint asked.

"I'm lookin'."

"Let's split up."

"Hurd's a big fella," Reckon said, "and Lee's real small. They make an odd lookin' couple."

"Let's take a quick look and meet up back here," Clint said.

"Right." The two men split up, leaving their horses behind so they could go on foot. Clint didn't see anyone who fit the descriptions Reckon had given him, but he did see someone he recognized.

Sitting at a picnic table, stuffing his face with fried chicken, was Kit Boone.

Chapter Twenty-Two

"I heard about this picnic, came lookin' for you, and when a lady offered me some fried chicken I accepted. After all, I had been on the trail a while, and was hungry.

Boone had aged since Clint last saw him, but then he was sure the same applied to him. Daniel Boone's great-grandson had been in his late twenties when Clint last saw him. Now in his early thirties, the man had filled out some in the chest, shoulders, and face.

"It's good chicken," Boone went on. "Set yourself a spell and have a piece."

"I don't have time right now, Kit, and neither do you," Clint told him. "We have work to do."

Boone put his piece of chicken down and said to the lady who had given it to him, "I'll come back later for more."

"Any time, Mister," the young woman told him.

As he had Clint walked away Boone said, "Pretty little things around here."

"I agree with you, Kit," Clint said, "and there'll be time for that tomorrow."

"Okay," Daniel Boone's tall great-grandson said, "What're we doin'?"

Clint explained the town's problem, which he had taken on as his own.

"I don't understand," Boone said, finally. "If they do this every year, why ain't they been caught, yet?"

"That's a question I've been asking myself for days," Clint said. "What's wrong with the people in this town?"

"What's wrong with the people in every town that leads to this one?" Boone asked.

"That's one of the things we're going to find out," Clint said. "But before we can solve that, we need to keep these kids safe."

"All right," Boone said, looking around, "which kids?"

"That's a real good question, Kit," Clint said. "For now, all of them."

When Clint and Boone reached Deputy Johnny Reckon, Clint made the introductions.

"Did you find the Hatfields?" Clint asked.

"I did," Reckon said. "All of 'em. They were sittin' at a table, eatin'."

"With all their kids?" Clint asked.

"Yep."

"Then we have to look elsewhere," Clint said. He looked at Boone. "Where's your horse?"

"In the livery," Boone said, "but he's spent."

"We'll rent one for you," Clint said. "Come on."

***

They got Boone a dusky dun that suited him and rode out again.

"Where we goin', Clint?" Reckon asked.

"The Porter place," Clint said. "I want Boone to look at the ground."

"For what?" Reckon asked.

"Sign," Clint said. "Something to indicate a gang with horses and wagons was, or is, in the area."

"Why the Porter place?" Reckon asked.

"Because Porter's a big man around here, and he's not very anxious to help keep the kids safe. I want to know why."

They rode onto Porter ranch property and Boone started studying the ground.

After a few hours Clint asked, "Anything, so far?"

"Indications of ranch hands," Boone said. "Or drifters passin' through. But nothin' like what you're lookin' for."

"Let's keep looking," Clint said. "Johnny, where was that line shack we looked at?"

"This way."

***

Boone rode the area around the line shack.

"Nothin' here," he said, after examining the ground.

"Where to next?" Reckon asked.

"Let's head back to town," Clint said, feeling frustrated.

They rode toward Temple City, but halfway there Boone shouted, "Hold up!"

Clint and Reckon turned.

"Look here," Boone said.

They rode back to him.

"A lot of horses passed this way, and at least two or three wagons."

"Going which way?" Clint asked.

Boone pointed west.

"That way."

"What lies that way, Johnny?" Clint asked.

"Well . . . the Porter ranch."

"You mean, ranch land, or the actual house?" Clint asked.

"No, we're on Porter land," Reckon said. "I mean the actual house. It's that way."

Clint looked at Boone.

"Let's follow the tracks. You take the lead."

Chapter Twenty-Three

They followed the trail until it took them within view of the house and barn.

"It goes right down there," Boone said. "To the barn."

"Sonofabitch!" Clint swore. "No wonder Porter doesn't want to help."

"I don't get it," Reckon said.

"The gang either works for or with Porter."

"Holy crap!"

"This is our first break," Clint said.

"Are we gonna ride down there?"

"Boone and I are going to creep down there on foot," Clint said. "You stay up here and keep watch. If anything goes wrong, you get back to town and tell the sheriff."

"But what if you need help?" Reckon asked.

"You get out of here, Johnny. Go back to town and you tell the sheriff. Understand?"

"I understand."

As Clint and Boone dismounted and started out on foot, dusk was falling. They could hear fireworks from town and could see some explosions in the air.

"You know who likes fireworks?" Boone asked.

"Who?"

"People who haven't been in a war."

"True."

They got low as they approached the back of the barn. When they reached the back wall, they searched it for gaps, where they could see inside, but there were none.

"Leave it to a man like Porter to use his money to have a barn built right," Clint said.

"Let's get around front."

When they got there, they saw the wagon tracks leading into the barn.

"Hopefully there are some kids inside," Clint said in a low voice.

Boone looked across at the house, and the ground between there and the barn.

"Nobody's around," he said. "Maybe they're all in town for the festivities."

"If that's the case, then there's nobody here," Clint said.

"We might as well take a look."

Clint nodded, and they moved towards the closed doors. They each grasped one and swung them open.

The barn was empty.

Clint stared at the empty interior while Kit Boone studied the ground.

"They were here," Boone said. "Horses, wagons, and in this corner the tiny footprints of children—a lot of them."

"They can't travel fast with that many kids," Clint said.

"From what you've told me the question is, have they snatched kids from Temple City yet? If not, then they're still here."

"You should be able to follow these tracks right to them, right?"

"I figure."

"Okay," Clint said, "But first, if nobody's around, I want to get a look inside the house."

"What for?"

"Some indication about where they're taking these kids," Clint said. "If we could get there first, we could surprise them."

"Then let's go and have a look."

***

Once outside the barn Clint turned and waved to Johnny Reckon so the young deputy would know all was well. Then they headed for the house.

"Is there gonna be anybody else in the house?" Boone asked.

"I don't know," Clint said. "A man as wealthy as Porter is bound to have some servants, but they could all be at the picnic. Let's be careful, anyway."

When they reached the house, they decided to try the front door, and found it locked.

"That figures," Clint said, "Let's go around back."

In the rear of the house, they found a door that led to the kitchen. Clint tried the door, found that they could probably force it.

"He uses his money to build a solid barn, and install a good front door, but he's cheap with the back door," Boone said.

Clint put his shoulder to the door, pushed, and it popped open. They stepped into the kitchen and closed the unharmed door behind them.

"Let's look around," Clint said.

"For what?"

"I don't know," Clint answered. "A desk, maybe."

"Okay."

"Split up. We'll meet back here in fifteen minutes."

"Right."

Chapter Twenty-Four

Ten minutes in, Clint found what appeared to be Porter's office. He also encountered an old black gentleman with a gun. As he walked through the door, the old man raised the gun.

"Easy, friend," Clint said.

"What do you want?"

"I'm just looking for some information," Clint said.

"What kind of information?"

"Do you work for Mr. Porter?"

"I run his house."

"Are there any others working here?"

"Just the cook, and she's at the picnic."

"What's your name?"

"Cyrus, Suh." The old man's hand shook as he pointed the gun, Clint felt the weapon was getting heavy in his hand.

"Well, Cyrus," Clint said. "I believe your boss is a bad man involved in stealing children. I'm hoping to find something in that desk to tell me what he's doing with them."

Cyrus dropped the hand holding the gun.

"Why didn't you say so?" he asked. "Somebody has to stop this man. Maybe that someone is you, Suh." Cyrus moved around from behind the desk. "Go ahead and look."

"Thank you, Cyrus."

Clint went around behind the desk, and while he went through the drawers, he asked Cyrus some questions.

"How long has your boss been doing this?"

"About five years, Suh."

"And do you know why?" Clint asked. "I mean, what he does with the kids?"

"I don't know, Suh," Cyrus said. "But I know that he pays a man named Trevor Henry to lead a gang for him."

"Trevor Henry?"

"Do you know him, Suh?"

"I've heard of him," Clint said. "But the Henry I heard of was a bank robber for many years—"

Clint stopped short when he saw something in the center top drawer of the desk. At the same moment Boone appeared at the door, gun in hand, and pointed it at Cyrus.

"No, don't" he snapped. "He's with us."

Boone lowered his gun.

"We were supposed to meet in fifteen minutes," he said.

"I know," Clint said. "I ran into Cyrus, who runs the house for Porter. He wants someone to stop his boss, so he let me look through the desk."

"And did you find anythin'?" Boone asked.

"I found this," Clint said, raising a sheet of paper. "It's a contract between Wayne Porter and the captain of a ship called The Traveler."

"A ship?" Boone asked.

"Apparently," Clint said, "Porter has a shipment to put on this boat."

"And go where?" Boone asked.

"It doesn't say," Clint said, "but it does note where the ship is leaving from."

"And where's that?"

"Galveston."

"That's a pretty long ride," Boone said. "Do we know when the ship is leaving?"

"No," Clint said. "Cyrus?"

"I don't know, suh."

"Well, there's one good thing," Boone said.

"What's that?" Clint asked.

"We can definitely get there before they do," the tracker said.

"Looks like I won't need you, Kit," Clint said, "now that I know where I'm going."

"Since I'm here," Kit Boone said, "maybe you wouldn't mind if I tagged along."

"I'd be glad to have you," Clint said. He put the paper back in the desk. "Cyrus, I don't need to tell you to keep this a secret. We were never here."

"Suh," Cyrus said, "I will clean the place so that the Mister never knows you were here."

"Thank you, Cyrus."

"Suh," Cyrus said, "if you can stop Mister Porter, then I say thank you."

Clint and Boone started for the door. Cyrus walked them to the front, where Clint stopped and turned.

"Cyrus," he said, "one more thing."

"What's that, Suh?"

"Did you ever see who was in the barn?"

"No, suh," Cyrus said, "I only saw Mr. Henry comes into the house."

"And did you see whoever was in the barn leave?"

"No, Suh," Cyrus said. "They must have left this mornin' like everybody else—the hands, the foreman, and Mr. Porter."

"I see," Clint said. "Again, thank you, Cyrus."

They left the house and made their way back to where Deputy Reckon was waiting.

"Anythin'," the young man asked, as they mounted up.

"Quite a bit," Clint said. "We'll tell you on the way."

"On the way where?"

"Back to town."

Chapter Twenty-Five

They found the sheriff at the picnic, with both hands full of fried chicken. They approached the table and Boone grabbed a piece.

"Clint?" Reckon said.

"Go ahead and eat, Johnny."

Clint sat next to Sheriff Cade and grabbed a chicken leg. Over their heads fireworks were going off, lighting up the sky.

Clint explained how they followed a trail to Porter's house, found indications that the gang had been in Porter's barn, and then what they found inside the house.

"Galveston?" Cade said. "They're gonna put these kids on a ship?"

"That's what it looks like."

"So you're heading there?"

"Hopefully," Clint said, "to keep any of those kids from boarding that ship."

"Are you going alone?"

"Boone's coming with me."

"Even though there's no tracking to be done?"

"He doesn't care," Clint said. "He wants to save these kids."

"So what does this mean?" Cade asked.

"Either they've already grabbed them," Clint said, "or they'll grab them tonight during all the fireworks."

"And are we going to try to stop them?"

"If we can catch them at it, yes," Clint said. "Otherwise tomorrow I'm heading for Galveston to head them off."

Clint finished his piece of chicken and stood up.

"There are plenty of kids here," he said. "I'm going to walk around and talk to some of the parents, make sure they know where their children are."

"Good idea. I'll come along."

"Why don't you stay here and watch everyone," Clint said. "You might notice something."

"Like what?"

"Like somebody you don't know hanging around and watching the kids."

"Good idea," Cade said, "I'll tell Johnny to do the same."

"Boone'll be here if you need him," Clint said.

"Good."

Clint started making rounds of other tables, spoke to parents whose kids were playing around or watching fireworks. According to all of them, they knew where their children were. Also, none of the parents in attendance had children under ten.

Could the gang be raiding the homes of families not attending the picnic and fireworks? It would take all night for Clint, Sheriff Cade, Deputy Reckon and Kit Boone to visit each family's home to find out.

Clint returned to the table where he had left Sheriff Cade, found the man standing there, keeping a sharp eye out.

"Over the past few years," he asked, "did you find out about missing children when the parents came to your office the next day?"

"Oh, yes," Cade said. "Even parents who claimed they watched their children carefully found them missing the next morning."

"And no one has complained so far."

"No, no one has."

"So the gang hasn't struck, yet," Clint said. "If we had enough men to fan out, we might be able to stop them."

"That would make it necessary to get volunteers," Cade said, "and that's not going to happen."

"Then there's only four of us," Clint said. "That's not enough to cover the entire county."

"Not near enough."

Clint shook his head.

"I can't imagine families staying here in Temple City after children went missing the past few years."

"I've spoken to many families after each of the past few years, and they insist they can watch their kids without having to leave their homes."

"Then they're foolish," Clint said, "and they'll pay the price. You know, if there weren't small children involved, I'd say these people are getting what they deserve."

"Any other ideas, then?"

"Yes," Clint said. "Have you seen Wayne Porter here?"

"No, why?"

"I think if we stick a gun in his face, we might be able to get him to talk, considering what we found at his house."

"There is a big fireworks display scheduled for midnight," Cade said. "In past years he's attended. I don't see why this year would be any different."

"All right, then," Clint said. "When he shows up, we can brace him."

"Let's remember," Cade said, "he's a big man around here. He'll have a lot of people standing up for him, even if it's only because they fear him."

Clint studied the lawman for a few moments, wondering if he was one of those people.

"I tell you what," Clint said, "leave it to Kit Boone and me to confront him."

"Look, Clint, it's not that I'm af—"

"No, no," Clint said, "I think we might be able to force him to talk if you're not involved. He won't be able to hide behind the law."

"Okay," Cade said, after a moment, "then when he arrives, I'll make myself scarce."

Chapter Twenty-Six

As midnight approached, Clint began to scan the picnic area for Wayne Porter. Instead, he spotted the foreman, Leo O'Neil. He found Sheriff Cade and walked up to him.

"I see Leo O'Neil, but not Porter."

"The big fireworks display is about to start," Cade said. "Porter doesn't usually miss that."

"Maybe I should check with the foreman, see what he has to say."

"Sounds good," Cade said. "Still want me out of it?"

"Yes," Clint said. "I'll call on you if I need you."

"I'll be ready."

Clint nodded and walked over to the foreman.

"Adams," O'Neil said, as if surprised to see him.

"Where's your boss, O'Neil?" Clint asked. "He's going to miss the big show."

"Mr. Porter has seen a lot of fireworks," O'Neil said. "He's a little busy, at the moment."

"Really?" Clint asked. "With the child stealer, Trevor Henry?"

"I don't know who you mean?"

"You know," Clint said. "The man who was using your barn to hide his men, and the children he had already stolen. Now he's out there stealing children from Temple City."

"I don't know—"

"Cut the crap, O'Neil!" Clint snapped. "Henry's adding to his collection and getting ready to deliver them to Galveston."

"Galveston?" O'Neil asked. "Why Galveston?"

Clint considered himself a good judge of people. It seemed to him O'Neil was really surprised.

"You didn't know about Galveston, did you?" Clint asked.

"Not a thing," O'Neil said. "They're takin' those kids to Galveston?"

"That's the plan."

"What for?"

"To put them on a ship."

"To where?" O'Neil asked.

"That I don't know," Clint said. "I figure they've already sold the kids and somebody's waiting for them, or they're looking to sell them when they get there."

O'Neil looked disturbed.

"Come on," Clint said. "You knew your boss was selling children, didn't you?"

"Not puttin' them on a ship," O'Neil said. "Where could he be sellin' them?"

"Overseas," Clint said.

"But . . . for what?"

"Slaves," Clint said.

"I thought we fought slavery in the war," O'Neil said.

"We did, in this country," Clint said. "Slavery is still big business in Europe, maybe Australia."

"They'd send those kids over there?"

"What did you think they'd do with them?" Clint asked.

"Get 'em good homes, I guess."

"O'Neil," Clint said, "those kids had good homes. They weren't stolen just to get them another one."

"Then they're just sellin' them to make money."

"That's pretty much it," Clint said. "Seems like most of Porter's money comes from selling these children into slavery."

Leo O'Neil shook his head.

"I've been a fool," he said.

"Don't be so hard on yourself," Clint said. "Porter's probably paying you well."

"Not that well," the man said. "After all, I'm just the foreman of his ranch. And like you pointed out, he's making most of his money in other areas."

"Do you know where he is now, O'Neil?" Clint asked.

"I thought he was gonna be here," O'Neil said. "I guess he's off somewhere with his hired child stealers."

"That's what I'm afraid of."

Chapter Twenty-Seven

While most oohed and aahed at the fireworks display, Clint and Sheriff Cade watched, feeling frustrated. Undoubtedly, while the sky was being lit up, children were being snatched, maybe even from their homes. Clint and the lawman knew they would have to wait til morning to find out just how many had been taken.

"With your friend, Boone, you should be able to track them," Cade said.

"That's true," Clint said, "or we could ride ahead and beat them to Galveston."

"And then what?"

"Wait for them at the docks, catch them loading the kids onto the ship."

"Just the two of you?"

"I might be able to recruit some law there," Clint said.

"I could send a telegram, give you some sort of official standing."

"That would help," Clint said. "That would make more sense than trying to take them on the trail, where we'd be outnumbered."

"You don't even know by how many," Cade said. "And you won't be able to recruit any help from the people in this town."

"What I'd like to do before we leave is put Porter's ass in one of your cells."

"We'd have to prove he was involved," Cade said.

"His foreman would talk."

"You said O'Neil knew about Porter's ranch business. He'd be guessing about everything else, in the eyes of the law."

"What about the houseman, Cyrus?" Clint asked. "He could tell you what he's seen."

"I don't know how much weight his testimony would carry," Cade said. "Especially against a man with Porter's reputation."

"Then I need to keep those kids from being loaded on that ship."

"If you send me a telegram that you've got proof about Porter's involvement, I'll toss his ass in a cell."

"I'll get proof," Clint said, looking up at the fireworks. "I think I've had enough of this. I'm going to get a drink at the Bent Axle."

"I'll stick around here a bit longer," Cade said.

"I'll see you in the morning, before I head for Galveston."

Still feeling frustrated, he headed for town and the saloon.

**

Wayne Porter waited in a clearing outside of town, where he and Trevor Henry had agreed to meet. From there he could see the fireworks display. In the midst of a huge burst of reds and yellows, he heard a horse approaching. In moments Trevor Henry rode into the clearing, along with his man, Lyle Kent.

"Is it done?" Porter asked.

"We got what we could," Henry said.

"We need a load of thirty," Porter said. "What do we have after tonight?"

Henry looked at Kent for the answer.

"We've got thirty-one," Kent said.

"Good, good," Porter said. "I want you to head out early for Galveston tomorrow. Before daylight, if you can."

"We'll be ready to go," Kent assured him.

Porter didn't like the fact that it was Kent answering most of the questions. Trevor Henry seemed to be looking at the fireworks, with a blank look on his face.

"Henry!" Porter snapped.

"Yeah, what?" Henry asked, taking his eyes from the sky.

"Are you going to be ready?"

"We're ready," Henry said.

"You better get there in time," Porter said.

Henry didn't respond, and Kent said, "We'll make it."

As Henry and Kent turned their horses to ride away, Porter shouted, "Kent!"

The man paused, turned his horse back around.

"Yes, Sir?"

"Henry's losing it," Porter said. "I don't care if he doesn't come back from Galveston. Do you get my meaning?"

"I get it," Kent said, and rode off after Henry.

Porter was now sure that, after this load, Kent was going to be his man.

***

Clint entered the Bent Axle and found it mostly empty. The bartender looked bored, and Honey was sitting at a table with two other saloon girls.

"Beer," Clint said to the bartender. As the man set it down, Clint asked, "The fireworks display is taking all your customers, huh?"

"Pretty much."

"Why aren't you out there looking at it?"

"I was in the war," the man said. "I seen enough explosions."

The batwing doors opened, and Clint saw another customer enter.

"Beer," Kit Boone said to the bartender. Then he turned to Clint. "Thought I'd find you here."

"Had enough fireworks?" Clint asked. "And chicken?"

"A belly full of both," Boone said. "I guess we didn't find out anythin' tonight, huh?"

"We'll find out in the morning just how many kids were taken," Clint said. "Then we'll head out."

"Trackin' 'em, or beatin' them to Galveston?" Boone asked, as the bartender set his beer down.

"I think I'd like to track them and get a look at how many we're dealing with."

"Sounds like a good idea."

"Once we know how many there are, we'll ride ahead and beat them to Galveston."

"Can we get some help when we get there?" Boone asked.

"We'll check in with the local law and see what they can do. Sheriff Cade's going to send a telegram ahead."

"Hearin' from a lawman ought to get us some help," Boone said.

"We'll have to wait and see," Clint said.

Chapter Twenty-Eight

"Ten," Sheriff Cade said when Clint entered his office the next morning. "Ten kids."

"That many?" Clint asked.

"Actually," Cade said, "that's the smallest amount in five years. I think parents were actually watching their kids last night."

"Not all of them," Clint commented.

"So when are you leaving?" Cade asked.

"I'm heading for Galveston," Clint said. "Kit Boone is coming with me."

Kit Boone was waiting out front on his horse when Clint came out.

"Ready?" he asked Clint.

Clint mounted his Tobiano and said, "Ready."

They rode out of town, heading to Galveston.

***

Porter had been out most of the night, waiting for word on this year's Fourth of July roundup. The total of ten kids was a disappointment, but at least this year's load was on its way to Galveston. Even the presence in town of the Gunsmith could not stop it from happening.

As he entered his office the next morning, he stopped short. Something in the room did not look right.

"Cyrus!" he shouted.

It only took seconds for the black man to appear in the doorway.

"You called, Suh?"

"Has anyone been in my office?"

"Yessuh."

"Who?"

"Why, me, Suh. I wanted to keep it clean."

"No one else?"

"No, Suh."

Porter walked around behind the desk, opened the top drawer and looked inside, then closed it.

"All right," Porter said. "You can go."

"Yessuh," Cyrus said. "Mr. O'Neil is here to see you, Suh."

"Send him in."

"Yessuh."

Porter sat at his desk and waited for his foreman.

"Come on in, Leo," he said, when the man appeared in the doorway. "Have a seat."

"I won't be here that long, Mr. Porter," O'Neil said. "I'm quittin' as of today."

"I see," Porter said. "Do I get to know why?"

"I think you know," O'Neil said.

"Do I?"

"I don't approve of some of your business practices."

"But you're only supposed to be concerned with running my ranch," Porter said. "Why would you have a problem with anything else I'm involved in?"

"Let's not play games, Porter," O'Neil said. "I don't like what you're doin' with these kids."

"Kids?" Porter contrived to look confused. "What are you talking about?"

"Slavery," O'Neil said, "I don't like that you're sellin' children into slavery."

"And where did you get that information?"

"I'm not blind."

"Leo," Porter said, "who else have you discussed this with?"

"No one," O'Neil said. "This is between you and me, nobody else."

"So you haven't gone to the law?"

"I haven't," the ex-foreman said. "I figure I owe you that much."

"Well," Porter said, "that's good to know."

He opened a drawer, took out a .44 Remington, and shot Leo O'Neil in the chest. The man only had a moment to look shocked before he fell to the floor and died.

Cyrus appeared in the door, his eyes wide.

"Suh?"

"Mr. O'Neil tried to rob me, Cyrus," Porter said, replacing the gun. "Have a few hands come in and dispose of this body."

"Suh? Dispose?"

"Oh," Porter said, waving a hand, "they can bury him."

"Yessuh."

As Cyrus went off down the hall, Porter wondered if O'Neil had told the truth about talking to no one else about his slavery business.

Chapter Twenty-Nine

Since the slavers were heading for Galveston, Kit Boone and Clint headed south, as Kit picked up the trail quickly.

It was just a couple of hours since sunlight when Clint said, "How far ahead?"

"Maybe a couple of hours," Boone said. "I figure they headed out before daylight."

"If we're lucky, one of their horses will step in a chuckhole."

"There's no need for that," Boone said. "We can travel two or three times as fast as they can. We can make up the time quickly."

"Okay," Clint said, "but I want to see them, I don't want them to see us."

"Got it. We can do that."

"Then let's go."

Boone gave his mount his heels, and Clint followed.

***

One hour later Boone reined in his horse.

"What's up?" Clint asked.

"They got to be just ahead of us," Boone said. "We'll have to go easy from here, with no noise."

"Well, I'll keep quiet," Clint said. "Now tell the horses."

"All we have to do is move more slowly," Boone said. "They have several wagons."

"How can you tell that? By the tracks?"

"Clint," Boone said, "I can hear 'em."

***

Trevor Henry was riding at the head of the procession, with Lyle Kent alongside him. Behind them the three wagonloads of kids moved single file, with Henry's men on both sides. One man was driving each wagon, and Lily was riding in the first one.

"We're movin' too slow, Trevor," Kent said. "At this rate we won't make the deadline."

"Then speed it up, Lyle," Henry said.

"I'm gonna ride back and check on all the wagons," Kent said. "Make sure the men can pick up the pace."

"Go ahead, then," Henry said, sounding annoyed. "I want to keep going."

Kent wheeled his horse around and rode back to the first wagon.

"Lily, I wanna pick up the pace," he said. "Whataya think?"

"The kids are okay, so far," she said. "There's no tellin' how cranky they'll be when they get tired, so we might as well push 'em now."

Kent rode back to the other two wagons. There were many big, wide eyes watching him, but at the moment none of them were crying.

He rode back to the front.

"Okay," he said, "let's pick it up."

"These wagons make a lot of noise," Henry said. "If anyone's trackin' us, they're sure to hear us."

"I can send a man to watch our back trail," Kent said.

"Yeah, do that," Henry said. "If he doesn't come back, we'll know somethin's wrong."

"I'll send Perkins," Kent said. "He's our best tracker, front or back."

"Tell him if he sees anybody not to approach them, just come back and tell us."

"Right."

Kent wheeled his horse about again and rode back to Ted Perkins.

"Back trail, Ted," he said. "Just check it out, don't approach anyone."

"Gotcha."

Perkins turned and rode back the way they had come, and Kent returned to the head of the column.

"What do we do if somebody's trackin' us?" Kent asked Henry.

"Who's gonna be stupid enough to do that?" Henry said. "And if anyone *is* that stupid, we have twelve men to take care of them."

"What about a posse?"

"Lyle, we've been through this town for five years in a row," Henry said. "Has there ever been a posse?"

"No, but—"

"Don't worry," Henry said. "Perkins will be back and you can stop worryin'."

"I don't know," Kent said. "I keep thinkin' the town will eventually rise up and work together."

"Porter will take care of that," Henry said. "He's got Temple City under his thumb."

"What if they hire somebody to come after us?" Kent asked. "Track us?"

"If they do," Trevor Henry said, "it better be some-body good. If I have to kill somebody, I want it to be somebody good."

Chapter Thirty

"If they're smart," Kit Boone said, "they'll send somebody to check their back trail."

"If they spot us, we'll have a decision to make," Clint said. "And before that happens, I'd like to know how many we'll be facing."

"So we have to see them before they see us," Boone said.

"How do you suggest we do that?" Clint asked.

"We split up," Boone said.

"It's your play," Clint said. "You call it."

"You ride to the east a few miles, then head South. After half a day, head west again, and we'll meet up. By that time I should know some things."

"I get it," Clint said. "You're afraid I'll be seen, but you know you won't."

"Not unless they've got someone real good ridin' with them," Boone said.

"I doubt they'll have someone better than you," Clint commented.

"We'll have to see," Boone said. "Remember, ride back this way late in the day, and we'll meet up around dusk."

"You think you'll have enough by then?"

"I should."

"And if you run into somebody?"

"I'll deal with that if it happens," Boone said. "What I can't do is kill them, because that would give us away. I'd have to convince them that I'm just driftin'."

"Whatever you do," Clint said, "don't get killed."

"I'll do my best."

***

Ted Perkins rode back the way they had come, trampling some of the tracks they left behind them. He was an expert tracker who had scouted for the Army, as well as a wagon train, and was very good at his job. Much of what he did was by instinct, and at the moment his instinct was telling him someone was on their trail.

After riding for an hour or so, Perkins became convinced either his instinct was wrong and no one was trailing them, or his instinct was correct, and they were being trailed by an expert. But he wasn't prepared to ride back to the column and tell Trevor Henry he thought they were being followed. He had to know, for sure.

So he continued to ride.

***

Kit Boone knew how to be invisible on the trail. He blended into the background with no problem and saw the man who had been sent to check the back trail. The man was good, but Boone was better, so he watched while not being seen himself.

But the man kept looking around, so Boone knew he had the instincts of a tracker. He knew someone was out there, watching him.

Boone continued to watch, and eventually the man gave up and started riding on ahead to join the others.

***

"Someone's out there," Perkins told Lyle Kent, "but he's good. I didn't see him."

"Then how do you know he was there?"

"I felt him."

"One man?"

"More than one I would've seen."

"All right," Kent said. "Don't say anythin' to Henry. I'll take care of it. But keep a sharp eye out behind us."

"I will."

Perkins drifted to the back, and Kent joined Trevor Henry in front.

Chapter Thirty-One

Trevor Henry halted the column and ordered everyone to make camp for the night.

"Keep those kids together," he told Lily.

"We're gonna feed them, right?" she asked.

"Bread, beef jerky and water," Henry said.

"That's all?"

"It'll keep them goin'."

"And the rest of us?"

"Bacon-and-beans."

That suited Lily. She knew Del Brandon could do magic with bacon-and-beans.

Lily made sure the kids were fed, kept them quiet, and then went to have her own meal. Two men were watching the kids while she ate with the others at the fire.

"Who's watchin' the kids?" Henry asked.

"Lucas and Hallum. They're the youngest, so they can run down any of them who try to get away."

"Okay, listen up while you eat," Henry said. "Perkins says we've got a tail, but he hasn't seen him. We're assumin' its one man."

"What're we gonna do, Boss?" a man named Nolan asked.

"We're gonna flush him out and kill 'im," Henry said. "We don't want anyone followin' us all the way to Galveston."

"How many of us are gonna flush him out?" Nolan asked.

"I'll tell you that in the mornin'."

Henry walked off with his plate and coffee cup to eat away from the fire, and his men. The only one to follow him was Kent.

"How many men are you gonna send out?" Kent asked.

"Three," Henry said.

"Is that enough?"

"That leaves nine of us with the kids," Henry said. "Eight men, and Lily. We'll need all of us. Perkins can take two men and track this tail down."

"You think that's best?"

"Why? You don't?" Henry asked. "Are you question-in' my decisions?"

"No," Lyle Kent said, "I'm not doin' that, Trevor. I'm just sayin'—"

"Well, don't!" Henry said. "Just do what you're told, Lyle."

"Right, boss," Kent said, and walked away. He stopped when he came alongside Lily.

"How bad is he?" Lily asked.

"He's still makin' the decisions," Kent said.

"Yeah, but what do we do after Galveston?" she asked.

"We're gonna get those kids loaded onto the boat, and then we'll make up our minds, Lily."

She reached out and touched Kent's arm.

"I'll go along with whatever you decide, Lyle."

"We still got a long way to go before I have to make a decision, Lily."

"I just want you to know I'm with you," Lily said. "I don't have much confidence anymore in Trevor's ability to make rational decisions."

***

Clint found Kit Boone making a cold camp.

"Can't afford to make a fire," Boone told him.

"That makes sense."

Clint dismounted, unsaddled his horse and got him settled, then sat with Boone and shared some water and jerky.

"What'd you find?" he asked.

"One man," Boone said, "and a pretty good one, too. He knew what he was doin'."

"Did he see you?"

"No, but I saw him," Boone said. "I think he felt me, but I know he never saw me."

"So where is he?"

"He went back to his people," Boone said. "He's gonna tell them somebody's out here."

"What do you think their next move will be?"

"Oh, they'll send a few men out to find me—us. We have to decide, do we avoid them, or take them out?"

"Take them out," Clint said, immediately.

"That was a quick decision," Boone commented. "Why?"

"To send these people a message," Clint said. "Keep them looking over their shoulders."

"Until when?"

"Until we get to Galveston ahead of them," Clint said. "I want to be there waiting."

"I think we should take a look first, and see how many we'll be dealin' with," Boone suggested.

"We'll do that," Clint said. "Get a head count, and then ride on ahead. We'll leave them to worry about whether we're behind them or in front."

"There's no way they could know that we know they're goin' to Galveston," Boone said.

"True," Clint said. "So if we take out some of their men, they'll be looking behind them the whole way."

"I'll take the first watch, and wake you in four hours," Boone said. "We should get an early start."

"No argument from me," Clint agreed.

Chapter Thirty-Two

When Trevor Henry woke the next morning, he heard children crying.

"Lily!" he shouted. "Shut them up!"

"They're hungry," Lily told him.

"Then feed 'em!"

"Water and Jerky?" she asked. "That's not gonna do it."

"Jesus Christ!" Henry swore, annoyed. "Tell Del to make them some bacon."

"Right."

"For all of us?" Lyle Kent asked.

"Yeah, sure," Henry said. "And then get Perkins and two more men out there after whoever's followin' us."

"You got it."

When Henry had a cup of coffee in his hand, he separated himself from the rest and drank it, staring off into space.

After Lily fed the kids, she went and stood next to Lyle Kent.

"Who are you sendin' out?" she asked.

"I'll let Perkins pick two men," Kent said. "He knows who he can work with best."

"Look at him, Lyle," Lily said, glancing over at Henry. "He looks lost."

"He's about done," Kent said.

Lily looked at him.

"What do you mean, exactly?"

"Porter doesn't want him back," Kent said. "He said he wouldn't mind if Henry didn't come back from Galveston."

"You mean . . . you're gonna kill 'im?"

"I think I'm gonna leave that up to him."

"What about the other men?"

"I think they all see that he's slippin'," Kent said. "They'll go along with whatever we do."

"I hope that's true," she said. "Some of these men have been ridin' with him for a while."

"We'll see," Kent said.

***

Clint woke Kit Boone and they both had a cold breakfast of jerky and water.

"How far ahead of us do you think they are?" Clint asked.

"Almost close enough to hear."

"I don't hear a thing."

Boone smiled.

"I mean close enough for me to hear."

"How do you figure they'll play it?"

"They'll send a few men back to try and find me," Boone said.

"We can avoid them, or take them out," Clint said. "Yesterday we were in favor of taking them out. What about today?"

"No change," Boone said. "We take care of them, then move ahead to see how many are left. Once we know, we can head for Galveston. But this is your call. I came to help you, remember?"

"I do."

"Then you call it."

"Let's see how many they send back," Clint said. "Three or four we can handle. Then we'll check how many are left."

"How many you figure?"

"With all the kids they've got in wagons, I'm thinking a dozen men, at least. For that many we'll have to get to Galveston ahead of them."

"And then what?"

"I don't know," Clint said. "We'll figure that out when we get there."

"Then let's break camp and get ready," Boone said. "They gotta ride back at first light."

"We'll be ready," Clint said.

***

"There," Boone said, pointing.

"I see them."

They spotted three riders coming from the south.

"That's the tracker, riding in front," Boone said. "If we take him out, the other two would be lost."

"Bushwhack him?" Clint said. "I can't do that, Boone."

"Then the other way to do it is to let them find me," Boone said. "And you get the drop on them."

"Before they can get off a shot," Clint said.

"That's the way I'd like it," Boone commented.

"Okay," Clint said, "let's go."

"I'll take point," Boone said. "When they come for me, you come for them."

"Got it."

***

"What's that?" Paul Gregory asked Perkins.

"That's our man," Perkins said.

"Let's get him," John Dylan said.

"That's just what he wants," Perkins said.

"How do you know?" Gregory asked.

"Because yesterday I couldn't even see him," Perkins said, "and now he's right out in the open."

"So he wants us to come for him," Gregory said.

"Right, again."

"So what do we do?" Gregory asked.

"We're gonna wait 'im out."

Chapter Thirty-Three

Kit Boone knew what was going on. He was waiting for them to make a move, and they were waiting for him. His mistake was in letting them see him. He was going to have to play this differently.

He rode a couple of miles with the three men watching him. He was sure that Clint was also watching all four of them. He only hoped Clint would figure out what he was doing.

Boone found an outcropping of rocks and rode around behind them.

He never came out . . .

***

"Where is he?" Dylan asked. "Where'd he go?"

"He disappeared," Gregory said.

"He's there," Perkins said, "only now he's not lettin' us see him."

"So whatta we do?"

"We head back."

"Without gettin' him?" Dylan asked. "We got orders."

"We got orders to get 'im," Perkins said. "We're gonna get him to follow us so we can all get 'im."

***

When Clint was sure he wouldn't be seen by the three men, he rode to join up with Boone.

"What's going on?" he asked.

"They changed plans," Boone said. "I think they want us to follow them."

"Can we get close enough to take them out?" Clint asked.

"Not without the shots being heard."

"How about if we do it without firing a shot?"

"And how would that go?"

"Well," Clint started, "we'd have to ride . . ."

***

Perkins, Gregory and Dylan were riding to rejoin Trevor Henry and the others.

"Anybody behind us?" Gregory asked Perkins.

"Nobody I can see," Perkins said, "but I can sure feel 'em."

"So are we leadin' them back to Henry and the kids?" Dylan asked.

"Why not?" Perkins said. "Let Henry have the pleasure of killin' them."

"He ain't gonna lose it?" Gregory asked.

"Ain't you noticed, he's losin' it already?"

The three men continued to ride, careful not to go fast enough to lose their tail.

***

Boone led Clint on a ride that took them ahead of the three men but did not catch up to the main column.

"There," he said, pointing to an outcropping of rocks. "We'll climb up there and drop down onto them. Hopefully, we'll take 'em without a shot."

Clint and Boone rode around behind the rocks to leave their horses hidden, then climbed on top.

"I'll take the one on the right and the middle, you take the other one," Boone said.

Clint didn't argue, as he was allowing Boone to call the play.

"Get ready!" Boone hissed.

They waited for the three men to come right beneath them, and then dropped down from the rocks.

As planned, Boone took two men off their horses, while Clint took one. All five men went sprawling, but Boone and Clint quickly reclaimed their balance.

Boone had his knife in hand, used it to cut the throat of the first man. He had more respect for the second man, who had been the one looking for him, so he simply slammed his knife butt into his head to knock him out.

Clint rolled as he fell and leaped on the back of the man he had taken off his horse. Rather than use his gun butt, he grabbed a rock and slammed it into the man's head.

One was dead, two were unconscious.

"Roll 'em over," Clint said. "I want at least one alive."

"You've got two," Boone said, pointing, "but this is the one you want. He's good at what he does."

"Get a canteen off one of their horses," Clint said.

Boone fetched a canteen and gave it to Clint. He uncapped it and poured some water on the man's face. He sputtered awake and stared at Clint and Boone.

"You awake?" Clint asked.

"I am."

"Who are you?"

"I said I'm awake," the man said, "I didn't say I'm alert. Gimme a minute."

Chapter Thirty-Four

They rolled the dead man off to one side, propped the other unconscious one against the rock, tied and gagged him so he would be taken care of when he woke. They allowed the third man to clear his head, but not enough time to formulate a plan.

"My name's Clint Adams, this is Kit Boone."

"Adams?" Perkins asked. "The Gunsmith?"

"That's right," Boone said.

"What's your name?" Clint asked.

"Perkins."

"Who are you working for, Perkins?"

The man tried to take a moment to think, but Clint pushed him.

"We know Porter's behind all this child stealing," he said, "but who's actually doing it? And who's taking them to Galveston?"

"You know about Galveston?"

"And the ship," Clint said. "And we're going to get there ahead of your people. But we'd like to know who we're dealing with."

Perkins turned his head.

"Your name's Boone?"

"That's right," Clint said. "He's Daniel Boone's great grandson."

"No wonder I couldn't see you," Perkins said.

"Perkins," Clint said, "we need some answers, and if we don't get them, there's no point in keeping you alive."

Perkins looked over at the dead man with his throat cut.

"Ask," he said.

"How many men are there?"

"There were eleven men and one woman. Now there's nine, altogether."

"Who's the leader?"

"A man named Trevor Henry."

Clint looked at Boone, who shrugged. Neither of them had ever heard of him.

"But he may not be the leader for long," Perkins added.

"Why's that?" Clint asked.

"He's losin' it," Perkins said.

"How do you mean?"

"I mean a few of us think he's loosin' his mind," Perkins said.

"So if that's the case, who would take over?"

"A man named Kent, probably. Lyle Kent. Right now, he's number two."

"And who watches the kids?"

"A woman named Lily."

"How many kids?"

"I dunno," Perkins said, "Maybe twenty-five."

"Do you know when they need to be in Galveston?" Clint asked.

"I know they're in a hurry, but I don't know the exact date."

Clint looked at Boone and said, "Whatever the date is, we've got time to beat them there."

"No doubt."

Both men looked at Perkins.

"What are you gonna do with us?" the man asked.

"We're going to leave you here, nice and trussed up."

"At the mercy of coyotes and buzzards?"

"Oh," Boone said, "the two of you will work yourselves free, eventually."

"And when you do," Clint said, "you better head the other way."

"On foot?"

"Oh, you might encounter your horses somewhere along the way," Clint said. "If not, you'll come to a waterhole, or a town somewhere along the way."

"Unless you'd rather we just kill you both right out," Boone offered.

"No, no," Perkins said, "we'll take our chances with the critters."

"Don't show up in Galveston, whatever you do," Clint warned him. "If you do, you'll be dead."

"Got it. You gonna leave us any food or water?"

"We're going to camp here," Clint informed him. "We'll feed you before we go and leave you your canteens."

"That's generous of you," Perkins said, and Boone knew he meant it.

Clint fetched their horses, while the mounts belonging to the other three had wandered off. They made camp, this time with a fire, and had some beans and coffee. They left the two men's hands untied so they could eat, then bound them tightly for the night.

Sitting at the fire Boone said, "I think we should kill 'em."

"I know you do, but I can't just execute them like that," Clint said. "They won't get in our way."

"I hope not. I'll take the first watch, wake you in four hours."

"We have a head count," Clint said. "Come morning, we'll just head for Galveston."

"We can beat them there by a day or two," Boone said. "That'll give us time to get ready."

Boone left the two outlaws bound and gagged when Clint turned in. He didn't want to talk to anyone during the night.

Chapter Thirty-Five

In the morning Clint stuck to his word, fed the two men, gave them coffee, then trussed them up again.

"You sure about this?" Perkins asked, before Clint tied his gag.

"Very sure," Clint said. "You'll be fine."

"Mmm-mmm-mm-gggfff," Perkins said.

"What?"

Clint tugged the gag down.

"You gonna leave us our guns?" the man asked.

"I'm afraid not," Clint said. "If and when you encounter one of your horses, you might find a rifle."

Perkins accepted that with a fatalistic shrug.

Clint and Boone saddled up and left the two men, tied up and sitting back against the rocks. There were already buzzards circling for the dead one, which they had pushed off to one side. Clint and Boone decided the man's friends could bury him when they finally got loose.

"I'm going to take a ride on ahead and see if I can confirm the head count," Boone said. "Then we can circle them and head for Galveston."

"I'll hang back," Clint said.

"Good," Boone said. "Less chance we'll be seen that way."

Clint started out at a canter, while Boone kicked his horse into a trot.

***

It was less than an hour later when Boone reappeared on the horizon. Clint reined his Tobiano in and waited.

"Perkins told the truth," Boone said. "I count eight men, a woman, and three buckboards with about twenty-five kids."

"How do the kids look?" Clint asked.

"Worn out."

"And the men?"

"All armed to the teeth," Boone said. "The woman's wearin' a gun, as well."

"The two of us against nine guns, to keep those kids off that ship."

Boone grinned at Clint.

"We got 'em right where we want 'em."

"Let's head for Galveston, then," Clint said. "We might as well get set up."

***

They took a circular route around the column of wagons and got ahead of them. When they had some distance between them

Boone slowed down to talk.

"I've got a suggestion," he said.

"What?"

"Let's take them on the trail instead of waiting in Galveston."

"I appreciate the confidence," Clint said. "But if we try to take them on the trail, the kids are going to get hurt, maybe killed."

"Okay, good point," Boone said. "Galveston it is."

"Have you ever been there?" Clint asked.

"A couple of times. You?"

"Once."

"Did you meet the law?"

"I did, but I doubt they have the same sheriff they had six years ago."

"By this time, they might even have a more modern police department."

"That wouldn't be bad," Clint said. "We'd be able to get more help, that way."

"Well," Boone said, "we'll find out when we get there."

***

"Where the hell are they?" Henry demanded.

"They may have run into more than they bargained for," Lyle Kent said.

"Relax, Trevor," Lily said.

"Relax?" Henry bleated. "Perkins is a good man, maybe our best. If he ran up against somethin' he couldn't handle—"

"That may not be it," Kent said. "There are a lot of reasons he's not back yet. Let's just wait and see what happens."

"Goddamnit!" Henry swore and walked away.

They had stopped only to rest the horses and see to some of the kids.

"He's really losin' it," Lily said.

"He just has to keep it together long enough for us to get these kids on the ship," Kent pointed out.

"Lyle," she said, lowering her voice.

"What?"

"Can't you just kill 'im now?"

"No," Kent said. "We need him to deal with the captain of the ship."

"Damn," she said, "it just would've been easier that way."

"I didn't know you were so bloodthirsty."

"Idiot!" she snapped. "It just would've been better for him!"

Chapter Thirty-Six

Galveston was larger than the last time Clint had been there and was split into different sections, but the only part they were really concerned with was the docks.

They rode directly there and dismounted. The Gulf of Mexico stretched out beautifully ahead of them, but something didn't fit the picture.

"Most of these boats don't look like they can float," Boone said.

"I don't think they call them boats," Clint said. "They're ships."

"They don't look good enough to be called ships."

"No, they don't."

"What's the name of the one we want?" Boone asked.

"The Traveler."

They walked along the docks, reading the names on the sides of the ships.

"It's not here," Boone said.

"If it's going to pick up a shipment of slaves, it probably docks and departs in record time."

"We don't know what day they're supposed to be here, so we don't know when it's dockin'."

"Maybe somebody does," Clint suggested.

"The law?"

Clint nodded.

"Might as well head there next."

They walked back to their horses and mounted up.

***

They found that Galveston had a sheriff's office and a modern police department. They decided to try the sheriff first. They dismounted in front of the office and entered. There was one man who looked to be in his sixties seated behind a desk.

"You gents look like strangers," the man said.

"We are, Sheriff."

"Then the only reason you'd come to see me is if you're lookin' for trouble."

"I'm afraid that's the case," Clint agreed.

"Well, I'm Sheriff George Fisher," the man said. "Who are you?"

"My name's Clint Adams, this is Kit Boone."

"Adams? The Gunsmith? What the hell are you doin' here?" Fisher asked.

"We're looking for a ship, called the Traveler."

"Ya gotta look down by the docks, for that."

"We did," Clint said. "It's not there, yet."

"What makes you think it's comin' in?"

"We were tracking a band of slavers here, decided to come ahead of them," Clint said. "That's the boat they're delivering their load to."

"Load of slaves?"

"Kids," Clint said, "a load of children."

"Jesus, kids? How small?"

"Five, six."

"How many?"

"At least twenty-five."

"How many slavers?"

"Nine."

"You two can handle nine guns?"

"If we have to," Clint said. "But some help would be nice."

"What, from me?" the lawman asked. "I been the law here for five years, and all they let me do is shoot dogs and serve papers. You want help you gotta go to that newfangled police station they got hereabouts."

"I thought that might be the case," Clint said, "but I wanted to try you first."

"I appreciate the thought," the lawman said, "but there ain't nothin' I can do for ya."

"Just tell us where the police station is," Clint said . . .

***

They followed the sheriff's directions to the police station and dismounted in front of a two-story granite building.

"I don't like these places," Boone said.

"Not crazy about them myself," Clint said, "but they might come in handy this time."

"I'll leave all the talkin' to you, then," Boone said, as they ascended the stairs.

They entered the building, which was much like stations Clint had seen in Denver, San Francisco and New York. A uniformed officer with three stripes sat manning a large desk.

"Can I help you gents?" the middle-aged man asked.

"Yes," Clint said, "there are three wagons loaded with children who are being sold as slaves, heading for your docks. We need your help to free them and catch the slavers."

The man stared at them for a few seconds, then said, "Oh, uh, I see. Just, uh, wait a minute."

Chapter Thirty-Seven

Clint and Boone waited while the man disappeared into the building. When he returned, he had a man in a grey suit with him.

"Mr. Adams?" he asked.

"That's right." Clint shook the man's hand. "This is Kit Boone. His great-grandfather was Daniel Boone."

The tall, middle-aged man raised his eyebrows.

"Is that right?"

"It is."

"And you claim to be the Gunsmith."

"Why would I claim to be the Gunsmith if I wasn't? I'd be painting a target on my back, wouldn't I?"

The policeman chuckled and said, "Yes, you would be, at that. My name is Lieutenant Boland. If you'll both follow me, we can talk in my office."

Clint and Boone followed the man into the bowels of the building until they reached a small office.

"Have a seat, please," the man invited. "It's a little cramped, but it'll do."

They all sat.

"Now what's this about a slave ring?"

***

Boland listened to Clint's tale attentively, without interruption.

"So you believe the gang is coming here with the children to load them onto a ship," he said, when Clint was finished.

"We have the name of the ship," Boone said. "The Traveler."

"The Traveler," Boland repeated. "Never heard of it." He sat back in his chair. "So what is it you want us to do?"

"We're going to try and take those kids away from nine guns," Clint said. "We could use some help."

Boland nodded.

"So you want some of my men."

"At least half-a-dozen should do it," Boone said. "We can't let those kids get loaded onto that ship."

"And how many kids are we talkin' about?" Boland asked.

"About twenty-five is the word we got," Clint said.

"From who?"

"One of the men working for Trevor Henry."

Boland frowned.

"I don't know that name, either."

"Neither did we," Clint said. "Look, what do you say, Lieutenant?"

"I don't know," Boland said. "we'd be taking your word for all of this, Mr. Adams. When will they be arriving?"

"Any day now," Clint said. "We made sure we got here ahead of them."

"I'll have to check this with my chief," Boland said. "It's hard to believe some old legend of the old West would be involved in something like the slave trade."

"We're interested in stopping it," Clint pointed out.

"Where will you be staying?"

"We don't know," Clint said. "We pretty much just arrived."

"Go over to Magnolia Street and stay at the May-flower. They've got their own livery stable. I'll contact you there."

"Soon, I hope," Clint said.

"As soon as I can," Boland said, standing. "Gentle-men, I'll show you out."

They followed Boland back to the lobby and front door.

"You'll hear from me soon, gents," the man said, and went back into the building.

Clint and Boone stepped outside.

"He doesn't believe us," Boone said. "Why would that be?"

"Maybe he doesn't believe we're who we say we are," Clint said.

"Like you said," Boone pointed out, "who'd lie about somethin' like that?"

"Let's get a hotel room and see to the horses," Clint said, "then get a good meal. I don't think we have to watch for Trevor Henry and his slavers to arrive until at least tomorrow."

They went down the front steps, mounted their horses and rode out.

***

They took the policeman's advice and went to the Mayflower Hotel. Once they each checked into their own room, they had their horses taken to the livery behind the hotel.

"We'll take our things to our room," Clint told the clerk, "but after that, we need a good steak."

"There's nowhere better than right here, Sir," the clerk said, "in our dining room."

"All right," Clint said, "we'll take your word for it and give it a try."

"You won't be disappointed."

168

Clint and Boone went to their rooms with their rifles and saddlebags, then came back down and met in the lobby. They walked to the entrance of the dining room and saw that it was about half full.

Clint asked for a table in the back and he and Boone sat and ordered their meals.

Chapter Thirty-Eight

Clint's steak and Boone's pheasant were both cooked perfectly. Getting a good meal in Galveston was not going to be a problem. But more than that, they had the problem of twenty-five or thirty children to deal with, whether or not the police agreed to help them.

They had a pot of coffee afterward and sat there to relax and discuss the task ahead of them.

"If the police don't believe us, and don't agree to help us," Boone said, "we'd either have to go it alone, or hire ourselves some help."

"It'd be hard to find good enough men in such a short time," Clint said. "I'm also concerned about another thing."

"What's that?"

"Sheriff Cade told me he'd send a telegram ahead to the local law, here."

"And did he?" Boone asked

"I don't know," Clint said. "Neither the sheriff nor the lieutenant mentioned it."

"Maybe we should ask."

"If Cade didn't send one, I have to question whether or not he was involved all along."

"So you think the only person you can trust is me," Boone said.

"That's for sure."

After the coffee, they paid their bill and went out to the lobby. One look out the front door showed darkness had fallen while they were eating.

"There ain't much we can do now," Boone said. "Goin' down to the docks in the dark wouldn't be smart."

"No," Clint said, "we'd be out of our element."

"So whatta we do?"

"Let's go out and get a beer?"

"Not here in the hotel?" Boone asked.

"We ate here," Clint said. "Let's get a drink somewhere else."

"I'm with you."

They left the hotel and started off down the street. After two blocks they found a likely looking saloon called The Hull House Saloon. It was quiet rather than boisterous, like a couple of the others they had walked past had been. And as they entered, they saw it was only half full.

"Gents," the bartender greeted, "what can I get you?"

"Two beers, please," Clint said.

"Did I hear this handsome man say please?" a woman's voice asked.

Clint and Boone looked on their right, saw a woman in a green dress standing at the end of the bar. She had long, black and creamy, flawless skin.

"That's not a word we hear in a saloon very often in Galveston," she continued. "That tells me you fellas aren't from here."

"You're right about that, Ma'am," Boone said.

"Oooh, nobody around here calls me ma'am, cutey," she said. "My name is Florence—and never Flo."

"You got it, Florence," Clint said. "My name's Clint and this is Kit."

"It's nice to meet you gentlemen," Florence said. "And because you've brought good manners to a mannerless place, your first beers are on the house."

"Is that in your power to do?" Clint asked. "Give away free drinks?"

"The lady owns the place," the bartender said.

"In that case," Clint said, as he and Boone raised their glasses, "thank you very much."

"Wow," Florence said, "please and thank you. You boys are going to spoil me."

"We'll do our best," Clint said. "And can we buy you a drink."

"Eric, you heard the gents," Florence said, "Champagne. The good stuff."

She came down the bar and joined them, with her long flute of champagne.

"What brings you gents to Galveston?" she asked.

"We have some business here," Clint said.

"And your business, does it involve guns?"

"What makes you ask that?" Boone asked.

"You both carry guns, and looks like you know how to use them," Florence said, then added to Clint, "especially you."

"We're looking for some people," Clint said. "Let's leave it at that."

She raised her glass and said, "Have it your way, gents." She drained her glass. "And thank you for the drink."

"Any time, Florence," Clint said.

She started away, then turned back.

"You fellas need a suggestion for a place to stay?" she asked.

"We have rooms," Clint said. "We're at the May-flower."

"Well," Florence said, "not the best in town, but pretty good. I hope you're successful with your business."

"She's quite a woman," Clint said to the bartender.

"You have no idea," the man told him.

Chapter Thirty-Nine

After two beers at the Hull House Saloon, Clint and Boone went back to their hotel to turn in. They wanted to get down to the Galveston docks nice and early.

They rose early and met in the dining room for breakfast, which was almost as good as their dinners were the night before.

"If it wasn't for the goddamn slavers I might be here to sample more of the food around town," Clint said.

"I doubt after we're done here that either one of us is gonna wanna stick around," Kit Boone said, "or ever come back. This is not gonna be fun."

After breakfast they decided to leave their horses where they were and walk back to the docks to see if the Traveler had docked.

After they had walked the length of the docks, they saw that the ship still was not there.

"Is this ship gonna pull in just in time to load those kids?" Boone wondered out loud.

"Not if we have anything to say about it," Clint said. "Let's see what the dockmaster knows."

Rather than skirting the docks they walked to the dockmaster's office. As they entered, they found a beefy, red-faced man shouting at three others.

". . . and if it's not done right, you three are gonna be out of jobs tomorrow. Now get out!"

The three dockworkers slunk from the room, and the man turned to face Clint and Boone.

"What can I do for you?"

"We're looking for a ship," Clint said.

"We've got a lot of ships here," the man said. "You gotta be more specific."

"It's called The Traveler," Clint said.

The man stopped shifting papers on his desk and looked up at them.

"You two aren't seamen," he said. "Why do you want The Traveler?"

"We're interested in its cargo," Clint said.

"I don't know what that is, off hand."

"Slaves," Clint said. "Child slaves."

The man scowled.

"That's ridiculous. Not on my dock."

"We're not sayin' you were aware of it," Boone said, "but it's happenin'."

"No it ain't."

"Not if we can help it," Clint said.

"Who are you guys?" the big man demanded.

"I'm Clint Adams, this is Kit Boone," Clint said. "We were following the slavers until we realized they were coming here. Then we rode ahead of them. We found out they're delivering the kids to The Traveler. Can you tell us when that ship docks?"

The man shifted some papers around on his desk, again.

"It's due in tomorrow," he said, "and due out the next mornin'."

"We'll be here to meet it," Clint said.

"Just the two of you?" the dockmaster demanded. "You're gonna handle the slavers and the crew?"

"Hopefully we can handle the slavers before the crew ever gets involved," Clint said. "What happens if the load doesn't get on the boat?"

"It's a ship, not a boat," the man said. "And they'll leave without it."

"Then that's what we need to make happen," Clint said.

"I don't know how I feel about you messing with my ships and my schedule."

"What's your name?" Clint asked.

"I'm Max Spearman."

"Max, one way or another, we're getting those kids away from those slavers, and we're not letting them on that ship."

"Just so long as you don't mess with my schedule, I don't care what you do."

"What about the Traveler's cargo being slaves?" Boone asked.

"Like I said," Spearman answered, "don't mess with my schedule and I don't care what the ships are carrying. Just as long as they come in and go out on time."

"That's mighty big of you," Boone said.

"Oh, one more thing," Clint said, on the way to the door. "Where will The Traveler be docking?"

Spearman checked his beloved schedule.

"Dock four."

"Thanks."

The dockmaster turned his attention back to his work.

***

Clint and Boone found dock four and drew hard looks from nearby dockworkers. Clint recognized two of them from the dockmaster's office. They were being yelled at.

"That dockmaster's a hard case, huh?" Clint asked the men.

The men looked at him and Boone.

"He likes things done his own way. When he doesn't get it, he hits the ceiling."

177

"He hits the ceiling anyway," the other man said.

"Tell us," Clint said, "is he an honest man?"

"He has a lot of faults," the first man said, "but as far as we know, he's honest."

"Just don't mess with his schedule," the first man said, and they walked off.

"Now what?" Boone asked.

"Back to the hotel to see if we've heard from the lieutenant," Clint said.

Chapter Forty

They stopped at the front desk to ask the clerk if there were any messages.

"Sorry, Sir," the man said. "Nothing."

"Thanks."

They stepped away from the desk.

"This doesn't surprise me," Boone said. "I didn't like that Lieutenant much."

"Neither did I," Clint said.

"So we'll do this with just the two of us?" Boone asked.

"We could," Clint said, "but I think we should give the sheriff one more visit."

"You think you can convince him to help?" Boone asked.

"If not," Clint said, "maybe we can get a suggestion or two for some help."

"Doesn't hurt to ask," Boone agreed.

They left their horses in the hotel's livery stable and caught a horse drawn streetcar to the sheriff's office.

"Back again," Sheriff Fisher said, from his desk. "Have you thought of a way I can help you?"

"Lieutenant Boland was no help, at all," Clint said.

"So it's the two of you against all the slavers," Fisher said.

"Unless you can suggest some help," Boone said.

"You want me to give you some guns for hire?" Fisher asked. "This isn't the Texas you know. There are no gunfighters here. I mean, *I'm* considered a dinosaur."

"Understood," Clint said.

"But," Fisher continued, "I think I might have two guys for you."

"We need them by tomorrow," Clint pointed out.

"Two blocks from the docks there's a saloon called The Rusty Hook," Fisher said. "Meet me at nine, and hopefully I'll have them there for you."

"That's fine."

"But remember," Fisher said, "it's up to them if they wanna work with you."

"We get that," Boone said.

"And don't walk into the Hook with any kind of attitude," Fisher said. "Because everybody in that place has an attitude."

"We'll keep that in mind," Clint promised. "We appreciate the effort."

"I'm thinkin' about those kids," the lawman said.

"We all are," Clint said, and he and Boone left the office.

***

Just outside of Galveston, Trevor Henry stopped the column.

"I don't like this," he told Lyle Kent. "Perkins never comin' back with those other two means they're dead."

"Maybe," Kent said. "There's still time."

"There's no time!" Henry swore. "There's somebody comin' up behind us who's already killed three of our people."

Henry and Kent were standing together in front of their horses. Lily dropped down from her wagon and walked up to join them. The other men remained on their horses and aboard their wagons quieting the children.

"What's goin' on?" she asked. "Are we ridin' in?"

"The ship's due in tomorrow," Kent said. "We don't want to hang around and wait."

"We'll ride in tomorrow," Henry said. "And we'll load the kids right on."

"So we're campin' here?" she asked.

"Yes," Henry said. "Make camp, get the kids fed and bedded down." He looked at Kent. "Tell Del to feed the men."

"Right."

Henry turned and looked into the distance. For the first time he wished he had more men. If he did, he'd send a batch back to see what happened to Perkins and the others. Maybe find out who was trailing them.

A bit later Kent brought a plate of food over to Henry.

"Thanks."

"Still don't think there's a posse after us?" Kent asked.

"Cade wouldn't take out a posse," Henry said. "There's more likely to be some hired bounty hunters."

"What do you want to do?"

"We'll deal with them when they catch up," Henry said. "Meanwhile, we'll get this load onto the ship tomorrow. Go get your own food."

"Right."

Henry sat down and started to eat, staring off into the distance behind them . . .

***

Kent sat down next to Lily at the fire.

"Is he gonna make it?" she asked.

"He only has to keep it together until tomorrow," Kent pointed out. "After that we'll take care of him and head back to Temple City to make new arrangements with Porter."

"You and me?" she asked. "In charge?"

"Two heads are better than one," Kent said.

Kent lifted his coffee cup to toast their new partnership. Lily grinned, grabbed the front of his shirt and said, "I have a better way to toast us."

She pulled him away from the fire, into the brush.

"What the hell are you doin'?" he asked.

"Just shut up and watch."

Once they were hidden from view, she unbuttoned her shirt and peeled it off, then shucked her boots and undid her trousers. Lily Palmer wasn't a very good looking girl, but at the moment she was a naked one, and Kent's mouth fell open. Her skin was pale, her breasts small, but her nipples were dark and huge. He had been with many whores in the past, but he had never seen nipples like hers. He was fascinated.

Her face was plain, but from that point on it didn't matter what she looked like. In moments she had Kent's trousers down around his ankles, and his cock swung free. She had seen him once, naked in a swimming hole, and had been thinking about his big penis ever since then. This was her chance, and she wasn't going to blow it.

She started to undo his trousers and he grabbed her hands.

"You're crazy," he said. "What if the kids, or one of the men, sees or hears us?"

"They can't see us back here, and they won't hear us if we keep quiet."

She fell to her knees and quickly took his cock into her mouth. She sucked him avidly, and when he was rock hard, she released him from her mouth and got down on her back, spreading her legs and beckoning to him.

"Come on, Lyle," she gasped, "fuck me."

"You're crazy," he said, but hurriedly freed one leg from his trousers, leaving them bunched around his other ankles as he fell on her and drove himself into her, sealing their new partnership.

Chapter Forty-One

Once again Clint and Boone left their horses behind, but this time they caught a horse drawn cab to their destination at nine that evening.

When they told the driver where they wanted to go, the man turned in his seat and asked, "Do you fellers know where yer goin'?"

"We have a good idea," Clint said.

The man shrugged and said, "Suit yerselves."

He drove them down just past the docks to a desolate looking street.

"This is it?" Boone asked.

"Right in there," the man said, pointing. "You boys still got time to go someplace else to do yer drinkin'. I can take you to a few good places."

They got out of the cab and Clint said, "No, this'll do us."

"Good luck."

He drove away before they entered.

Clint and Boone entered the saloon, which was large but dingy inside. It was also noisy, although there was no gambling going on. Gambling usually caused at least half the noise in a saloon.

They stopped just inside the door to look around. Conversation stopped and they became the center of attention.

"Over here, gents," Sheriff Fisher called, waving from a table.

When the other patrons saw that they were meeting with Fisher, they relaxed and went back to their conversations. Clint and Boone walked over and joined Fisher at a table. Clint noticed the man wasn't wearing his badge.

" 'evenin', Sheriff," Clint said.

"Just call me Fisher, here," the man said. "I don't wave my badge in people's faces."

Clint and Boone sat down. Fisher waved and a beefy bartender appeared with three mugs of beer.

"You may not believe it," Fisher said, "but these glasses are clean."

"Glad to hear it," Clint said.

He and Boone took a drink and found the beer cold and refreshing.

"Where are the men you were tellin' us about?" Boone asked.

"They'll be here," Fisher said. "Just relax. It may look like you've been accepted here, but you haven't, yet."

"If you're a lawman, why are you accepted?" Boone asked.

" 'cause I'm one of them," Fisher said. "And they know that, as a lawman, I'm a joke."

"And you don't mind that?"

"Hey," Fisher said, shrugging, "I get paid, and I don't have to work on the docks. It suits me."

"Well," Clint said, looking around, "nobody seems to mind, so I guess it suits them, too."

"Ah, here's one of the men I was talkin' about," Fisher said, waving to someone.

The man who approached them was tall and slender, with a baleful face that Clint suspected had never smiled.

"Gents, this is Linc."

"Just Linc?" Clint asked.

"Just Linc," the tall man said. "Fisher says you're Clint Adams, the Gunsmith," They shook hands. "And you're related to Daniel Boone"

"Great-grandson," Kit said, shaking the man's hand.

"Have a seat," Clint said, "and a beer."

Linc sat and accepted a beer from the bartender.

"Fisher says you need help," Linc said. "Why would the Gunsmith need help?"

"I'm about to face nine guns," Clint said, "maybe more."

"And all he has to back him up is me," Boone said, "and I'm a tracker, not a gunfighter."

"But everything I've read about you," Linc said to Clint, "says you shouldn't have trouble with nine men."

"Well," Clint said, "you can't believe everything you read. And it's more than just a shootout. There are children involved."

"Children?"

"Maybe we better wait and tell Bishop, as well," Fisher said.

They all looked up at the shorter, slight man who was approaching.

"Bishop!" Linc said, with distaste.

"I guess I should've warned you," Fisher said to Clint. "These two don't like each other.

The approaching Bishop had a high forehead and pointed chin.

"Linc!" he said, when he reached the table. "What's he doin' here?" he asked Fisher.

"Sit down, have a beer, meet these gents, and we'll tell you," Fisher said. "Or rather, they'll tell you."

Bishop looked at them.

"Clint Adams," Clint said.

"Kit Boone."

"Adams?" Bishop asked. "The Gunsmith?"

"That's right," Fisher said. "Interested?"

Bishop looked at them all, scowled at Linc and said, "I'll have a beer."

Chapter Forty-Two

"Slaves?" Linc asked.

"Kids?" Bishop said.

"Yes," Clint said.

They both looked at Fisher.

"Don't look at me," Fisher said. "I can't do anythin'."

"But you're the sheriff," Bishop said.

"That don't matter," Fisher said. "You know I'm a joke. A dog catcher."

"What about the police?" Linc asked.

"We talked to a Lieutenant Boland," Boone said, "No luck."

"Oh, he said we'd hear from him," Clint said. "But we haven't yet, and it's getting late."

"When will the children get here?" Linc asked.

"The ship is due tomorrow," Clint said. "We assume the children will also arrive, then."

"And be loaded onto the ship," Bishop said.

"Yes," Clint said, "unless we stop them."

"The four of us," Linc said.

"The sheriff says you're the two men who can help us," Clint said.

"If they can work together," Fisher said.

Linc and Bishop glared at each other.

"Well," Clint said, "I suppose we could use one of you."

"I'll do it," Linc said.

"No, I'll do it," Bishop said.

They glared again.

"Look," Fisher said, "why don't the two of you work together for the kids? You can hate each other after."

"We could use the help," Boone said.

"We ain't gunmen any more than you are," Bishop said to Boone.

"I'll take care of most of the gunplay," Clint said. "I'm going to need help on the docks. I don't know much about ships."

"Well," Linc said, "I guess we can help ya with that."

"We're pretty well known on the docks," Bishop said.

"In fact," Fisher said, "everybody on the docks knows these two can't stand each other, so they won't suspect they're workin' together."

"That might come in handy," Boone said.

"How well do you know the dockmaster, Spearman?" Clint asked.

"We both know Max," Bishop said.

"You have a run in with him?" Linc asked.

191

"He told us not to mess with his schedule," Clint said.

"Yeah, he means that," Linc said. "If he doesn't like you, he'll send some men after you."

"But they won't have guns," Bishop said.

"We won't give him any reason to send anyone after us," Clint said. "We just want to get those kids back to their parents."

"Well," Linc said, "you've got my help."

"Yeah," Bishop said, "mine, too, I guess."

"Then I'm buying beers all around," Clint said, and Fisher waved the bartender over with five fresh ones.

***

When the five men left the Rusty Hook, Clint told Linc and Bishop where they were staying.

"Well," Linc suggested, "I don't think we should meet anyplace else but here."

"That sounds like a good idea," Bishop said.

"Look at that," Fisher said. "You got these two agreein' on somethin' already."

"This place is two blocks from the docks," Linc said. "If the men you're waitin' for get there, you'll find us right here."

"I've got a better idea," Clint said. "This place open early?"

"It never closes," Fisher said.

"Let's all meet here in the morning," Clint said. "And then we'll split watches on the docks."

"Agreed," Linc said, and Bishop nodded.

"That, uh, doesn't include me, right?" Sheriff Fisher said.

"Don't worry, Sheriff," Clint said. "You've done everything we expected you to do."

"Then I'm going back inside," Fisher said. "I wish you all luck."

The lawman went back into the Rusty Hook.

"We'll see you both tomorrow," Clint said.

Linc and Bishop went their separate ways.

"You think those two will work together?" Boone asked.

"We can only hope so," Clint said.

***

Trevor Henry walked over to where Lyle Kent and Lily were sitting.

"Lily, go and check the kids."

"They're fine," she said.

"Check them, anyway!"

Lily stood up and walked off.

"Lyle, tomorrow you and he are gonna ride in ahead of everyone else," he said. "We're gonna make sure that ship is there."

"Whatever you say, Trevor," Kent said.

"I'm anxious to get rid of these kids tomorrow."

Henry walked back to his own fire, which he kept separate from everyone.

"I'm anxious to get finished with this whole thing," Kent said to himself.

Chapter Forty-Three

Clint and Boone got to the Rusty Hook at eight a.m., the next morning. As promised, the place was open. Inside they found Linc and Bishop eating breakfast at separate tables. It was obvious that neither man had a gun, but they both had a long, curved, metal hook with a wooden handle.

They stood inside the door, wondering which man they should join for breakfast.

"You fellas can sit over here," the bartender said, indicating a third table.

Clint shrugged and said, "Fine."

They walked to the table, and as they passed Bishop he said to them, "I'll work with Linc, but I don't hafta eat with him."

"That suits us," Boone said.

He and Clint sat, and the bartender brought them each a plate of bacon, eggs and potatoes with a basket of biscuits and a pot of coffee.

"This is unexpected from a saloon," Clint said.

"That's why the Rusty Hook is special," the bartender said.

When Sheriff Fisher walked in, he stopped and looked at the three tables.

"I'm gonna join you fellas," Fisher said, sitting with Clint and Boone.

"I thought you weren't getting involved?" Clint said.

"Hey," Fisher said, "I'm just here for breakfast."

The bartender brought him a plate and cup, then went back around behind the bar. There was no one else present in the place. The tables were close enough for conversation without shouting.

"Can we talk while we eat?" Clint asked. "Is that all right?"

"Fine with me," Linc said.

"Why not?" Bishop asked.

"We're expecting the slavers in today," Clint said. "That's because the ship is due today."

"You think they're gonna come drivin' in?" Linc asked.

"No," Clint said, "we expect them to send someone in advance, to check on the ship."

"That means you'll want someone in the dock master's office," Bishop said.

"Will he go along with that?" Clint asked.

"He will for me," Bishop said.

"And me," Linc added.

"Can one of you get him to put up with us in his office, as well?"

"Probably either one of us," Linc said. "For some reason he likes us both."

"So are you two the only ones who don't like each other?" Boone asked.

"That just might be the case," Fisher broke in.

All five men finished their breakfasts and pushed their plates away.

"Let's all sit together for a cup of coffee," Clint said, and they all agreed. Linc and Bishop joined Clint, Boone and Fisher at their table.

"Which one of you wants to start the day on the docks?" Clint asked.

"I'll do it," Linc said, then looked at Bishop, "if that's all right with you."

"No, problem," Bishop said. "I'll relieve you in three hours."

"I'll come in three hours after that," Clint said, "and then Boone."

"Even though I won't be in Spearman's office all day, I'll be around," Linc said.

"So will I," Bishop said. "You won't have any trouble findin' us when your slavers arrive."

"I better get over there, then," Linc said, standing. "See you all later."

The tall man went out the door.

"I know a bunch of the teamsters on the docks," Bishop said. "I'm gonna see what they know about this ship, The Traveler."

"Good idea," Clint said. "I'll see you there, later."

Bishop nodded to the three men and left.

"Well," Fisher said, "it looks like they're gonna work together."

"You doubted it?" Clint asked.

"Actually, I did," Fisher said, "but I knew each of them would be a help to you."

"They don't have to like each other," Clint said, "they just have to hate the men who enslave children."

"I hope they're right about the dockmaster cooperatin'," Boone said.

"He will," Fisher said. "He's known both men a long time."

***

"You want to what?"

"Sit in here with you."

"How long?" Max Spearman asked.

"All day, if we need to," Linc said.

"We?"

"Yeah," Linc said, "he, Bishop, Clint Adams and Boone."

"Clint Adams," Spearman said. "I spoke to him. Is this about that ship, The Traveler? And slaves?"

"Yeah," Linc said. "We want to be here when it docks."

"What's goin' on Linc?" Spearman said. "And why the hell are you and Bishop workin' together?"

"We don't like each other," Linc said, "but none of us want those kids sold into slavery. What about it, Max? Can we stay?"

"Why the hell not?" Spearman said. "As long as you don't mess with my schedule."

Chapter Forty-Four

Trevor Henry and Lyle Kent rode within sight of the Galveston docks.

"What's this ship look like?" Kent asked.

"How the hell do I know?" Henry answered. "The only boat I've ever been on is a riverboat."

"Well, there's a few ships there," Kent said. "What's the name of ours?"

"The Traveler."

Kent took a spy glass from his saddlebag to get a better look.

"I don't see that one," Kent said.

"It's supposed to be here today," Henry complained.

"Well, it's early," Kent said. "There's still time for it to arrive."

"Sonofabitch!" Henry swore. "We got here, the ship should've got here."

"What about gettin' paid?" Kent asked. "Do we have to go back to Temple City for that?"

"Porter will have someone here to pay us," Henry said.

"Okay, fine," Kent said. "We have to wait for that ship to get here. We can't bring those three wagonloads of kids to the docks to wait."

"No," Henry said, "we'll leave them just outside of town until the ship gets here, then drive them in."

"So do we just sit here on our horses and wait?" Kent asked.

"I need a drink," Henry said. "What about you?"

"Definitely!"

"Okay, we'll find a saloon and then take turns," Henry said. "One in the saloon, one watchin' the docks."

"Suits me," Kent said.

He needed time to figure out when and how he was going to kill Trevor Henry. He couldn't do it until after the kids were loaded onto the ship, and they got paid.

They both urged their horses into Galveston . . .

***

Linc decided to sit by the front window of the office and watch the dock. The slavers would not be able to load the kids onto the ship without checking in with Max Spearman first. This way he'd see everyone who approached the office before they got there.

So far all he was seeing were dock workers, carrying hooks identical to the one that was hanging from his own belt.

Men walked in and out of the office, but Linc recognized them all. They withstood the ire of Max Spearman, who praised no one during the course of a day, and pretty much growled at everyone.

Linc continued to watch until he saw Bishop approaching the office. He stepped outside to meet the man.

"Max says it's okay," he told Bishop, "as long as we don't damage his schedule."

"As usual," Bishop said. "No sign of anythin' yet?"

"No slavers, no ship," Linc said. "You get anythin' from the dockworkers?"

"Nobody knows anythin' about a ship called The Traveler," Bishop said. "Seems real odd. I don't think that ship has ever docked here before."

"Adams said these slavers have been operating for about five years," Linc said. "If they've been using Galveston all that time, then it looks like they've been usin' different ships."

"If they've been at it for five years," Bishop said, "Max has to know about it."

Linc frowned.

"I hate to think Max is in with slavers," he said.

"I'll wait inside," Bishop said. "Maybe you should mention that to Adams."

"You're right, I will."

The Two men stared at each other, realizing this was probably the longest civil conversation they had ever had.

***

Linc found Clint and Boone in the Rusty Hook, where they had decided to wait. They each had a beer in front of them, as it was now early afternoon. Likewise, there were now other patrons seated at the bar, and at a few tables. Linc sat.

"Anything?" Clint asked.

"Just a thought," Linc said. "You said these slavers have been at it for five years. Have they been using Galveston all that time?"

"That we don't know," Clint admitted. "Why?"

"Well, if they have, then Max Spearman has to be in on it."

"The dockmaster?" Boone said. "That makes sense, but you and Bishop said you knew him."

"We said he knew us," Linc said. "And he's always seemed honest to us, but there must be big money in this slave business."

203

"I'd say so," Clint said.

"Well, Max likes money," Linc said.

"Then we better keep a close watch on him, as well," Clint said.

"Actually," Linc said, "we already are."

Chapter Forty-Five

Henry and Kent found a saloon called The Rusty Hook, but decided against it.

"It's too local," Henry said. "We'll stand out."

"They're all local," Kent pointed out. "Let's find a crowded, noisy one."

"This time of the day?"

"Or we could just sit and wait at the docks," Henry said.

Kent frowned.

"There's got to be a noisy place, somewhere."

They kept looking.

***

"Does Spearman have a wife? A family?" Clint asked Linc.

"He lives alone."

"So once we free the kids and take the slavers into custody, he could light out," Clint said.

"And go where?" Linc asked. "He practically lives on the docks. No, if we put an end to this slave business, he'll probably just walk off the end of one of the docks."

"Die rather than be caught?" Boone asked.

"Die rather than lose his job," Linc said. "His job's his life."

"Then why risk it for this?" Clint wondered.

"It may be his life," Linc went on, "but it pays him nothin'. He's workin' with the slavers for the money."

"All right," Clint said. "I'll relieve Bishop in a couple of hours. That'll put us at midday. I can't see the ship arriving after dark."

"You never know," Linc sad. "They could dock, load and depart in under an hour."

"Then we'll have to be ready for that," Clint said.

"Bishop's a little closer to Max than I am," Linc admitted. "He might get somethin' we can use."

"That'd be helpful," Clint said.

Linc stood up.

"Where are you off to?" Clint asked.

"Bishop talked with dockworkers and came up empty. A couple of them might tell me somethin'. I'll be on the docks."

"Okay," As Linc started for the door Boone asked, "Is that hook the only weapon you have?"

Linc moved his jacket aside to show a knife on his belt.

"And this. I don't like guns."

"As long as you're good with that," Boone said.

"I'm good with both of 'em," Linc said and left.

Boone looked at Clint.

"He's gotta get close with the knife or the hook," he said.

"I'm going to have to be as good as my reputation," Clint commented.

Boone grinned.

"Probably better."

***

Trevor Henry and Lyle Kent found a place called The Iron Maiden Saloon. It was crowded and noisy.

"This'll do," Henry said. "I'm gonna have a few drinks, then relieve you at the dock."

"Lily's gonna be watchin' for the signal to move in," Kent said. "I gave her my spyglass."

"Good," Henry said. "If you see the ship enter the port, come and get me. We can be there in minutes. I'll do the same."

"You got it."

Henry grabbed an empty table as Kent left the saloon. He ordered a beer and drank it, his mind wandering.

***

"Time for me to relieve Bishop," Clint said to Boone.

"I'll come along," Boone said. "Just to be around the docks."

"Suits me."

They left the Rusty Hook and walked to the docks. Boone veered off as Clint approached the dockmaster's office.

As Clint approached the office, the door opened and Bishop stepped out to meet him.

"Anything?" Clint asked.

"No," Bishop said. "Max is keepin' his mouth shut about The Traveler."

"Well," Clint said, "it looks like we'll all be on the docks from now til the ship arrives."

"And the slavers?"

"I'm sure they're nearby, watching and waiting," Clint said.

"I'll take a look around," Bishop said, "discreetly."

"If you spot them, point them out, but don't do anything," Clint said. "I want to wait until that ship arrives before we move on them."

"I understand," Bishop said.

"Okay," Clint said, "then I'll see you later." He entered the dockmaster's office.

Chapter Forty-Six

Lyle Kent saw the two men stop and talk in front of the dockmaster's office, then one walked in and one walked away. It looked like one man was taking over for another. He didn't like it, and thought he ought to let Trevor Henry know something was going on.

***

"I don't like this, you know," the dockmaster said.

"I know, you made that clear the first time we talked," Clint said. "But we're not doing anything to interfere with your schedule."

"You better not," Spearman said. "I don't know how you got Linc and Bishop to work together, or to join you, but I don't like it."

"Maybe if you knew something, and you told me—"

"I don't know nothin'," Spearman said, jabbing the air in front of Clint's face with a blunt finger. "Just stay out of my way."

Clint put his hands up and said, "Done."

He went over and sat at the window, as Linc and Bishop had done before him. From there he could look up the length of the dock where the office was. It was empty and, with any luck, this was where The Traveler would be docking if, indeed, Spearman was part of the plan.

***

Lyle Kent entered the Iron Maiden Saloon and walked to Trevor Henry's table.

"Already?" Henry asked. "I've only had one beer."

"Go ahead and have another," Kent said. "I just wanted to tell you what I saw."

He sat and explained while Henry listened. In the meantime, two fresh beers were brought to the table, and when Kent finished talking, he drank half of his down.

"So you think this was a change of watch you saw," Henry said.

"That's what it looked like to me."

"You recognize either of the men?"

"No, but one looked like a local dock worker. The other looked like a cowboy, complete with a gun and holster."

"You think he followed us from Temple City?" Henry asked. "And he's the one who took out Perkins?"

"I don't know what to think," Kent said. "I'm just tellin' you what I saw."

"Well," Henry said, "we better get back there."

"Both of us?"

"It's gettin' late," Henry said. "That ship's gotta be comin' in soon."

They both finished their beers and got up.

Outside, while they were walking to the docks, Henry asked, "You didn't see more than those two men?"

Kent shook his head.

"No, just those two."

"So the cowboy got himself a local to help him."

"An *unarmed* local," Kent pointed out. "I didn't see no gun."

"That's good," Henry said. "Because we've got plenty of guns."

***

It was only because he was keeping a sharp eye out that Boone saw the two men approaching the docks. But there was no way for him to get to Clint and tell him, so he continued to watch.

***

"I don't see anybody but locals," Kent said to Henry.

"Well, we know the one in the office ain't a local," Henry said. "Maybe there's another one around here, someplace."

"If we worry about too many, we'll never get this job done," Kent said. "However many men there are, we'll take care of them. And don't forget, we'll have the crew of the ship on our side."

"That's right," Kent said. He was impressed that, at the moment, Trevor Henry seemed as sharp as ever. "So what do you wanna do? Go and talk to the dockmaster while that cowboy feller is in the office?"

"Why don't we?" Henry said. "We can find out who he is."

"What if he's law, and he tries to take us?" Kent asked.

"Then we kill 'im," Henry said. "It's two against one. And if he's not law, we'll find out just who he is and what he wants."

"What if he's a bounty hunter?" Kent asked.

"Same difference," Henry said. "He's a dead man."

"All right, then," Kent agreed, "Let's do it."

Chapter Forty-Seven

When the two men made their way to the end of the dock and started for the office, Boone ran.

***

When the office door opened and the two men walked in, Clint knew the time had come. Max Spearman turned and looked at the men, and there was no sign of recognition on his face. Clint turned from the window and faced the men.

"What can I do for you two gents?" Spearman asked.

"I think you know," one man said. "You're the dockmaster, right?"

"That's right."

"We're waitin' for a ship to come in," the man said.

"The Traveler?" Clint asked.

The two men turned to face him.

"Who the hell are you and what're you doin' here?" one man asked.

"My name's Clint Adams, and I'm here to take all those children you've stolen home."

The two men exchanged a glance.

"You're the Gunsmith," one said. "Why do you care?"

"Because they're children," Clint said. "And they shouldn't be sold into slavery."

"So what do you intend to do?" one man asked.

"First," Clint said, "I want to find out who you men are?" But before they could answer Clint remembered something Cyrus, the houseman, had told him. "Wait, one of you is named Trevor Henry."

That seemed to surprise both of them.

"I'm Henry," the first man said.

"And you?" Clint asked the second man.

"That doesn't matter," Henry said. "You have no official standin' here, Adams."

"I don't need any official standing to shoot the two of you where you stand."

"You . . . you wouldn't do that," the other man said, his voice shaking.

"Relax," Henry said to the man. "He won't do it."

"Why not?" Clint asked.

"Because at the sound of a shot, all those children will be killed."

"You'd do that?" Clint asked.

"In a minute," Trevor Henry said. He turned to Spearman. "When will that ship be in?"

"Soon," Spearman said, "before dark."

214

"Good," Henry said. "Our cargo will be here, ready to be loaded."

"B-but . . . what about him?" Spearman asked, pointing at Clint. "If he really is the Gunsmith—"

"Oh, he is," Henry said. "I'm sure of it. But he won't do anything—or rather, he *would* do anything to keep those kids alive." He looked at Clint. "Ain't that true?"

Clint didn't answer.

"We're goin' out this door," Henry said. "If you've got any help out there, you better make sure they don't do anythin'." He looked at the other man. "Let's go."

Henry opened the door and went out, followed by Kent. Clint brought up the rear. He saw Boone at the end of the dock and waved him off. He hoped the wave would also keep Linc and Bishop from taking action.

Max Spearman stood in the open door, and Henry turned to look at him.

"Make sure that ship is ready for our cargo."

"It will be," Spearman promised.

Trevor Henry and Lyle Kent walked back up to the end of the dock. They exchanged a look with Boone, and then kept going.

***

After Henry and Kent left, Clint turned to Spearman. The two men stepped back into the office.

"Hey," the dockmaster said, "I didn't know who you was—"

"Forget it," Clint said. "We have to figure out a way to save those kids."

"B-but you heard 'im," Spearman said. "He'll kill 'em."

Clint turned as Boone entered.

"What happened?" Boone asked.

"That was Trevor Henry, the leader of the gang, and one of his men."

"Why didn't you take 'em?" Boone asked. "There was only two of 'em."

"At the sound of a shot, all those kids would've been killed."

"Jesus!"

"At least we know they're close enough to hear a shot," Clint said. "Now we have to figure out a way to take those kids without a shot being fired."

"We?"

"Yes," Clint said, "you, me, and the dockmaster here, Mr. Spearman."

"M—me?"

Chapter Forty-Eight

"What's goin' on?" Lily asked as Henry and Kent returned.

"The ship should be comin' in any minute," Henry said. "The dockmaster says it'll be before dark."

"Then when do we move?" Lily asked.

"Might as well be now," Henry said.

"We found out who was trailin' us," Kent said.

"Who?"

"Clint Adams."

Her eyes went wide.

"The Gunsmith? Why's he involved?"

"It doesn't matter," Henry said. "He can't do anythin', because he's worried about these kids."

"What did you tell him?" she asked.

"That if he makes a move to stop us, we'll kill the kids."

"Kill them?"

Henry nodded.

"All of them."

"Are you serious?" she asked.

"It only matters that he thinks I am," Henry said. "So let's get them loaded up and move out."

"Come on," Kent said to Lily, "I'll help you."

They walked over to where all the children were sitting on the ground.

"Get them loaded into the wagons," Kent ordered the men watching them.

"Yessir."

As the loading was going on, Lily said to Kent, "Is he serious? I mean, about killin' these kids?"

"Dead serious."

"If they're dead, we don't get paid," she said. "We better kill him before he does something rash."

"Whether he does or not is gonna be up to Adams," Kent said.

"Then I guess we'll have to kill him," Lily said.

"It may come to that," Kent said. "But as long as he thinks Henry will kill the kids, he'll cooperate."

"All right," she said. "I'm gonna leave this up to you."

"Then let's get them loaded," Kent said.

***

"You want me to what?" Spearman asked.

"You heard me," Clint said. "Can you do it?"

"Well," the man said, "once The Traveler is docked. But it'll be tricky."

Clint looked at Boone.

"Let's get Linc and Bishop," he said. "They can overlook the unloading."

"So then handling the slavers is gonna be up to you and me, again," Boone said.

"I guess so," Clint said. "When the shooting starts, I'll just have to try and take care of Trevor Henry first. The others might lose interest if he's dead."

"There's gonna be shootin'?" Spearman asked.

"Oh yes," Clint said, "there's going to be shooting."

"All of this is definitely gonna mess up my schedule," Spearman complained.

"Mr. Spearman," Clint said, "you just better hope you come out of this alive. Being dead would really wreck your schedule."

"Dead?"

"Just get to it," Clint said. "Make the arrangements."

Boone arrived with Linc and Bishop.

"Okay," Clint said, "this is what's happening . . ."

***

Clint and Boone were standing at the end of the dock when the wagons appeared, with Henry and Kent leading them. At the same time, they all saw the ship enter the port. The Traveler was a huge freighter, and Clint was impressed as he watched it dock. The crewmen ran about, each doing their appointed job in getting the ship secured.

Clint wanted to wipe the smug look off Trevor Henry's face as he led the wagons onto the dock, past Clint and Boone, up to the ship. Several crewmen came down the plank to meet the wagons.

"Get them onboard," Henry told them.

Lily and several men took the kids off the wagons and handed them over to the crewmen, who marched them onboard while Trevor Henry observed.

Also observing from the doorway of his office was Max Spearman, who was hoping against hope there would be no shooting.

While Clint and Boone watched the small children march onto the ship, Clint asked, "Are Linc and Bishop on board?"

"They are," Boone said.

"All right, then," Clint said. "We'll wait for the last child and then make our move."

Boone gripped his rifle and said to Clint, "Don't worry, I'm ready."

Chapter Forty-Nine

Henry watched as the last of the children boarded the ship, then turned to Kent and Lily.

"That's it," he said.

"Who pays us?" Kent asked.

"Don't worry about that," Henry said. "I'll take care of it."

They turned and saw Clint and Boone standing by the empty wagons.

"What do you want, Adams?" he asked. "It's over. You lost."

"Not quite."

Henry laughed.

"The kids are on the ship. That doesn't mean I can't kill them."

"Actually," Clint said, "it does."

Henry frowned.

"Whatayou mean?"

"If you think those kids are on that ship, go and have a look."

Henry frowned, then turned and ran up onto the ship.

"Where are those kids?" he asked a crewman.

"They ain't here," the man said.

"Whatayou mean they ain't here? I saw them get on."

"We took 'em on, and offloaded them on the other side, like we was told."

"Offloaded?"

"Onto another ship."

"What? Show me."

"Over here."

The crewman led Henry to the other side of the ship, where he saw a second ship just pulling away. On board that ship he could see all of the children, with two men, one tall, one smaller and slighter.

He turned to the crewman.

"Get them back here!"

"I can't."

"Ahhhh!"

Henry turned and ran back to the plank. At the bottom stood Clint and Boone, and beyond them Kent, Lilly and the rest of Henry's men.

"Kill them!" he shouted. "They took the kids. Kill 'em!"

A couple of the men drew their guns, but before they could fire, Clint drew, Boone pointed his rifle, and they both fired. Two men spun around when the bullets hit them and fell to the ground.

Lily grabbed for the gun in her belt, but Kent said, "Don't!"

He grabbed her arm, stopping her.

There were four other armed men, but they looked down at the two dead men and didn't go for their guns.

"Drop 'em!" Clint said. "Now."

The four men took their guns from their belts and dropped them to the ground.

"You, too," Boone said to Kent and Lily.

They both dropped their weapons.

"No! No!" Trevor Henry shouted. "I said kill them!"

But he could see it was no use.

"Come on down, Henry," Clint said. "You were right about one thing. It's over."

Henry thought about grabbing his gun from his holster, but the Gunsmith already had his gun in his hand. So he did the only thing he could think of. He turned, ran to the other side of the boat, and jumped off . . .

***

When the other, smaller ship docked, they took the children off.

"Did you see where he went?" Clint asked Linc and Bishop.

"We saw him jump off and hit the water. After that, nothing," Linc said.

"He could've drowned," Bishop said, "or he swam away."

"What's the difference?" Linc asked. "He's finished."

"No," Clint said, "I wanted to take him in. If he's still alive, I want him."

"What are you gonna do with all these kids?" Linc asked.

"Boone and I will take them back to Temple City," Clint said. "From there we'll get them to their parents."

"We're gonna need some men to drive the wagons," Boone said.

"Don't look at me," Linc said.

"Me, neither," Bishop said. "I ain't leavin' Galveston."

"Can you find us three men?" Clint asked. "We'll see that they're paid well."

"That can be arranged," Bishop said.

"Look there," Boone said, pointing to the end of the dock.

Clint looked and saw Lieutenant Boland with half a dozen uniformed policemen. The man must have had them being watched.

"Better late than never, I guess," Clint said. "Let's turn all these men and the lady over to them. Then I want to talk to the dockmaster."

***

After the police had taken the slavers away, and removed the two bodies, Boone and Clint went into the dockmaster's office.

"Now whataya want?" Spearman asked. "I did what you tol' me. I got you another ship."

"You did," Clint said. "Now I want to know where the money is you were supposed to pay the slavers."

"What money?"

"Come on," Clint said. "Somebody had to pay them after the delivery was made. There's nobody but you."

Spearman looked dejected, opened a drawer and took out a thick envelope.

"Somebody from the bank brought it to me,"

"From who's account?"

"That I don't know."

"Who else?" Boone asked. "Porter."

"I'm sure," Clint said.

"What do you want to do with it?" Boone asked.

"We're taking the children back to Temple City," Clint said. "We might as well return Mr. Porter's money."

"What about Henry?" Boone asked.

"I get the feeling we'll find him in Temple City, too," Clint said. "After all, he's going to want to get paid."

"He'll beat us there," Boone said. "But this time we have the kids."

"We'll work that out," Clint said, "but we better get moving."

***

Trevor Henry swam ashore and, by that time, had already decided what his next move would be. He laid there and caught his breath. He had to get a horse, and head back to Temple City. One way or another, Wayne Porter was going to pay what was owed.

Henry knew his mind was not as sharp as it once was. He didn't know what was happening to him, but he recognized lapse of memory when he had them, and he knew Lyle Kent and Lily had noticed, as well. His intent was for this to be his last job. He was going to collect his payment, not share it with anyone, and get himself to the best doctors to find out what was happening to him. And he knew he'd have to do this before Lyle Kent killed him—probably with the help of Lily Palmer. And probably at the order of Porter.

Clint Adams' appearance had ruined his plan, but he could still get to Porter and force a payment out of him. No doubt Adams and his man would be taking the children back to their parents. That would give Henry time to get to Porter.

All he had to do was dry off and steal a horse. Whatever else he needed, he could steal along the way.

Chapter Fifty

Temple City, Texas

When Clint Adams and Kit Boone arrived in Temple City once again, Boone asked, "What's first?"

"It's late," Clint said. "Let's get a drink, then a room and some sleep. We'll deal with everything tomorrow."

"I think I'm gonna get a room and go right to it," Boone said. "I'll see you in the mornin'."

"I'll meet you in the lobby at nine."

Kit Boone went to get himself a hotel room, while Clint went into the Bent Axle Saloon for a beer. He was greeted by Honey, who took him to a table and brought him a beer.

"Can you sit?" he asked.

"I'd be happy to," she said. "Did you save those kids?"

"We did," Clint said. "They'll be here in a couple of days, and we'll get them back to their parents."

"What will you do in the meantime?" she asked.

"The man we were after got away," Clint said. "We think he'll be coming back here to get paid."

"So you're waitin'?"

Clint nodded.

"Do you have a hotel room?"

"I'm getting one," he said, "right after this beer."

She smiled and said, "No, you're not."

***

Honey let Clint finish his beer, then took him to her room above the saloon.

"You can stay here with me, or there's an empty room down the hall."

"I think you know the answer to that," Clint said.

The room was decorated in bright colors, with a bedspread that matched the floral material of a large armchair.

"Sit in the chair and I'll take off your boots," she said. "You look tired."

"We rode hard a long way," he admitted.

She pulled off his boots and socks and then massaged his feet. When she reached for his gunbelt, he stopped her.

"Don't worry," she said. "I'll hang it on the bedpost. You can get to it easily."

He allowed her to remove it and drape it on the post, then she undid his belt, trousers and shirt, leaving him in his underwear.

"We can stop here and you can go to sleep," she said, "or . . ."

She backed up and tugged the dress she was wearing down off her shoulders, so that it fell to her waist. Those large, beautiful breasts sprang forth and made his decision for him.

So did the large bulge in his crotch . . .

***

Clint may have been tired, but he took the time to enjoy Honey's body before the two of them fell asleep. When he woke the next morning, she was down between his legs, thoroughly enjoying waking him by sucking him until he was long and hard. Then she mounted him and took him inside. She rode him hard, and with abandon, until he exploded inside her and she almost screamed . . .

***

Clint dressed while Honey watched him.

"What are you going to do today?" she asked.

"Finish this," he said. "Catch Trevor Henry and put Wayne Porter in jail."

She looked surprised

"You think Sheriff Cade will arrest Porter?"

"I know he won't," Clint said. "The sheriff was in on the whole thing."

She was even more surprised.

"How do you know that?"

"He told me he'd send a telegram to law enforcement in Galveston," Clint explained, "so they'd back my play. He never did that."

"It's gonna hit this town hard to find out that Porter was stealing the children."

"And selling them as slaves," Clint said. "This town is going to have to make do without Mr. Porter and his money, and with a new sheriff."

"Are you gonna kill them? And this Trevor Henry?"

"I'd rather send them all to jail, but . . . in the end it'll be up to them."

He strapped on his gun and grabbed his hat.

"Will I see you again?" she asked.

"When this is all over," he said, "definitely."

He leaned over, kissed her, and resisted the urge to put his hands on her naked body again. If he had, he may have never left the room.

Chapter Fifty-One

Clint met Boone in the lobby, and they went into the dining room for breakfast.

"Who first?" Boone asked. "Porter or the sheriff?"

"The sheriff," Clint said. "We'll get him to ride out to Porter's with us."

They finished their breakfast and walked to the sheriff's office. If Cade was surprised to see them, he hid it well.

"You're back," he said. "How did it go?"

"We rescued the kids and got most of the slavers arrested," Clint said.

"Most?"

"The leader, Trevor Henry, got away. We think he's on his way back here to get paid."

"By Porter?"

Clint nodded.

"Want to ride out there with us?"

"Why, sure," Cade said. "Why not?"

As they walked to the livery to get their horses, Clint said, "Somehow, your telegram never got to Galveston."

"Sorry about that," Cade said. "I sent it—"

"We're not blaming you," Clint said, cutting the man off. "It all worked out. Now we just need to get Henry and Porter."

"And get those kids back to their parents," Boone added.

They saddled their horses and headed out to the Porter ranch.

"What's Porter been doing these past few weeks?" Clint asked.

"Business as usual," Cade said. "Dinner at the Cattleman's Club. Nothing unusual."

"Nothing odd has happened?" Clint asked.

"Well, his foreman quit," Cade lied. He knew O'Neil was dead.

"O'Neil?" Boone said.

"Yes," Cade said, "left just after you did."

"Has he replaced him?" Clint asked.

"Not yet. The top hand has stepped in for the time being."

"Travis?" Clint asked.

"That's right."

"He struck me as a good man," Clint said, "not likely to go along with Porter's slavery business."

"You think Porter's still at it?" Cade asked.

"Not when he finds out we stopped him this time," Clint said.

"If he knows you know he was behind it, do you think he'll still be at his ranch?"

"He's just arrogant enough to try and brazen it out," Clint said. "We'll see when we get there."

***

Wayne Porter was sitting in his office when his houseman, Cyrus, came stumbling into the office, slamming into his desk.

"What the hell—" Porter started, but he stopped when Trevor Henry appeared in the doorway, gun in hand. The man was a disheveled mess, with a wild look in his eyes.

"Sorry, Porter," he said, "your man was a little reluctant to let me in."

"It's all right, Cyrus," Porter said. "You can go."

"No, no," Henry said, "I think he should stay. Just move into that corner, Cyrus, there's a good boy."

Cyrus did as he was told.

"Now I don't know if you've heard from your people in Galveston," Henry said to Porter, "but Clint Adams managed to completely ruin the deal at that end. In fact, he's on his way back here with all those children."

"I got a telegram saying the delivery wasn't made," Porter said, "but no details. Adams, huh? That figures. I guess we'll have to start from scratch."

"No, I don't think so," Henry said. "I made the delivery as I was supposed to. I want my money, and then I'm through."

Chapter Fifty-Two

Clint, Boone and Sheriff Cade reined in their horses in front of Porter's ranch house. As they dismounted, Clint looked around and found it odd not to see any ranch hands.

"Are they off on a trail drive?" he asked Cade.

"Not that I know of," the lawman said. "But they might be out on the range."

They mounted the stairs and knocked on the door. There was no answer.

"That's odd," Cade said, "Cyrus usually answers."

Clint reached for the knob and found the door locked.

"I'm gonna go around back and have a look," Boone said.

"Good idea," Clint replied.

Boone left the porch and trotted around the side of the house.

"Can we force the door?" Clint asked Cade.

"Not legally," the sheriff said. "Let me knock again."

This time he pounded his fist on the door. Anyone inside would have heard, but no one answered.

***

When Boone got around to the rear of the house, he saw a horse there. The animal had obviously been ridden hard and was still blowing. It was tied in front of a rear door, Boone looked through the window and saw the kitchen. He tried the door, found it open and entered. He was walking through the house when he heard a pounding on the front door. He went to answer it.

***

When the front door opened Clint found himself looking at Boone.

"The kitchen door was unlocked," Boone said, "and there's a horse tied back there—a horse that's been ridden a long way."

"Henry," Clint said.

"I'll bet."

"Let's find Porter."

"Let's not," Sheriff Cade said.

They both turned and found themselves looking down the barrel of his gun.

"Before we see Mr. Porter, I want your guns. Take them out easily, with two fingers, and drop them. Don't try to draw, Adams. I'll kill Boone before you get me."

"Go ahead, Clint," Boone said, "Kill 'im."

"No," Clint said, "not just yet."

He took his gun out with two fingers and dropped it. Boone did the same.

"I was wondering when you'd give yourself away," Clint said to Cade.

"What do you mean?" Cade asked. "You knew?"

"You never did send that telegram to Galveston."

"No, I didn't," Cade said. "Let's go down that hall to the right. We'll find Porter in his office."

"Why not?" Clint said. "Time to get this over with."

He led the way down the hall, with Boone behind him and Cade taking up the rear.

***

"You can't quit," Porter said.

"Why not?" Henry asked. "I'm sure you had Lyle Kent ready to kill me and take over. Now you can start fresh with someone else. All you have to do is pay me."

"But the delivery was never made."

"It was by me," Henry said. "I put those children on the ship. It's not my fault Adams took them off."

"Trevor, be reasonable—"

"I can't be reasonable, Porter," Henry said. "I'm losin' my mind. At least, some of it. I'm gettin' forgetful, at times. So you see, I've got other problems to take care of, and for that I need money."

"I don't have any in the house."

"I'm sure that's a lie," Henry said. "I'll bet you have a safe around here someplace. And I'll bet Cyrus knows where it is." Henry looked at the black man. "Cyrus?"

"Well, Suh—"

"Keep your mouth shut, Cyrus!" Porter said. "Or you're fired."

"That's all right, Suh," Cyrus said. "I was about to quit, anyway."

"That's a good man, Cyrus," Henry said. "Show me the safe and I'll give you a little bonus."

"He can show you where it is," Porter said, "but he can't open it."

"You're gonna do that, Porter."

At that point they all heard a pounding on the front door.

"I should get that," Cyrus said.

"Relax, Cyrus," Henry said, "let's see how long it takes whoever it is to get in."

Chapter Fifty-Three

When Clint came to the door of the office, he stopped.

"Keep going," Cade said.

"He might shoot me when I walk in," Clint said.

"That'd be too bad. Move!"

Clint entered the room, followed by Boone.

"Stop there!"

He saw Porter behind his desk, but the speaker was Trevor Henry, standing off to one side with a gun.

"You're pointing a gun at my chest, and someone else is pointing one at my back. Who do I listen to?"

"Who's behind you?" Henry asked.

"Sheriff Cade."

Henry frowned, as if he didn't recognize the name. He was momentarily confused.

"Get in here and shoot this bastard!" Porter shouted to Cade.

Cade rushed into the room. In the split second it took him to locate Henry, the other man shot him. Cade doubled over, dropped his gun, and fell to the floor.

"Now what?" Clint asked.

"You're the Gunsmith," Wayne Porter said. "Shoot him."

"That's kind of hard to do without a gun," Clint commented. "Are we interrupting something?"

"A negotiation," Trevor Henry said. He looked at Porter. "Before I forget, where were we?"

"He's crazy," Porter said. "Kill him."

Clint and Boone looked at each other. Boone's hand came out from behind his back and his knife flew across the room toward Henry. The slaver reacted quickly, ducking to one side and firing at Boone. At the same time, Clint dove for the gun the sheriff had dropped. He rolled, came up on one knee holding the gun, and fired at Trevor Henry. Henry grabbed his belly, all the air was driven from his body and his eyes bulged. As he slid to the floor, Clint looked at Boone, who was holding his side.

"You okay?"

"I'm hit," Boone said, "but I've had worse."

"We'll get you to a doctor." Clint looked at Porter. "You're coming with us."

"Where?"

"To town."

"What for?"

"There's a cell waiting for you there."

Again, the man asked, "What for?"

"For running a child slavery ring."

"You're not the law."

"Around here that doesn't seem to mean much," Clint said. "You had the law in your pocket. You're going to pay for your crimes."

"Look," Porter said, "you've got no proof. He's the slaver," he said, pointing at Henry, "and he was a crooked sheriff," pointing at Cade. "Now they're both dead. There's nobody to testify against me."

"There's him," Clint said, indicting Cyrus.

"Cyrus works for me."

"Not no more," Cyrus said.

Porter narrowed his eyes.

"You sonofa—who's going to take the word of a darky against mine?"

"A jury of twelve of your peers," Clint said. "With what Cyrus has to say, combined with what Boone and I know, I don't think there'll be much of a problem convicting you."

"I've got a lot of money in the house," Porter said. "It's yours." He waved a hand. "There's enough for all three of you."

"I can't answer for Boone or Cyrus," Clint said, "but you don't have enough."

"And not for me," Boone said.

"Me neither, Mr. Porter, Suh," Cyrus said. "You is a bad man."

"I guess that's it," Clint said. "Let's go. You're going to jail, right after I get Boone to a doctor."

Clint marched Wayne Porter out of his house, while Cyrus put Boone's arm around his shoulders and helped him.

The Independence Day Gang had run its last job.

On Sale Now!

THE GUNSMITH GIANT SERIES

For more information
visit: www.SpeakingVolumes.us

Upcoming New Release

J.R. ROBERTS

THE GUNSMITH

THE RED LADY OF SAN FRANCISCO
BOOK 478

**For more information
visit:** www.SpeakingVolumes.us

On Sale Now!

THE GUNSMITH *series*
Books 430 – 477

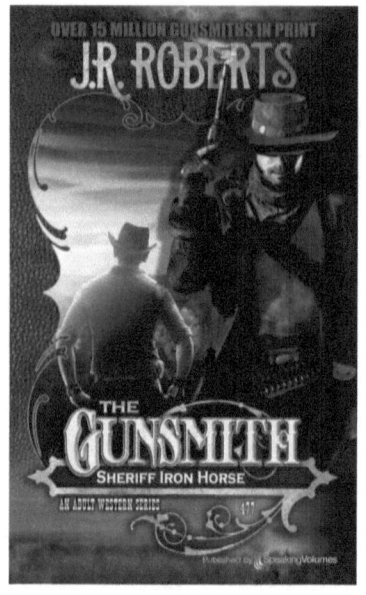

For more information
visit:

On Sale Now!

LADY GUNSMITH
BOOKS 1 - 9

For more information
visit: www.SpeakingVolumes.us

On Sale Now!

TALBOT ROPER NOVELS
ROBERT J. RANDISI

For more information
visit: www.SpeakingVolumes.us

.

www.ingramcontent.com/pod-product-compliance
Lightning Source LLC
Chambersburg PA
CBHW050502260626
47157CB00004B/1158